FROM A
DARK CELL

A novella by

Colin Alcock

Novels

Tuna on Tuesdays

A Darkness of Voices

The Spider Man

Novellas

Emilia's Sorrow

From A Dark Cell

**Compilations of
Short Stories and Flash Fiction**

Dandelion Days

The Schooling Chair

Colours in Darkness

First published 2022

This is a work of fiction.
Where names, characters and places appear, they are
either a product of the author's imagination or used fictitiously,
as are any events that occur in recognisable locations.
In such cases, any resemblance
to actual persons, places and events
is entirely coincidental.

ISBN No: 9798415837106

Website: colinalcock.co.uk

For Mary

Who has to suffer the first draft
of everything I write.

Five Dark Days

●●●

The floor is filthy with coal dust, a tacky grime running across one corner: just all hard concrete and cold. When there is light, it's a sharp glare from a single, bare bulb that casts harsh shadows of my body onto the dirt encrusted walls. There is nothing in the room other than a galvanised bucket, with a handle that clanks in loud echoes when I move it and a crude wooden lid over it that does little to stop the foul smell of excrement.

Little sound penetrates this space, just eight paces by five, with one locked door and a metal hatch in the ceiling, far out of reach, even when I tried standing on the upturned bucket. That was where coal or coke used to be delivered, I would guess. And where a faint glimmer comes in the day, through a thin gap where two, time-buckled flaps of the hatch are bolted across. If only I could reach those bolts, so tantalisingly too high.

I've lost count of the days I've been incarcerated. I can only remember waking up here and with my mind dull and confused as to how and why I have arrived in this unforgiving black hole. I've had meals brought to me, the only time the light is switched on, all too briefly, but I can't remember how many. Or what they were. Was it some Dickensian gruel? It tasted foul enough and if I am being drugged – as I am beginning to suspect – I can't taste with what, as I reluctantly spoon gagging mouthfuls. Disgusting as it is, I have to get back my strength, that much I know, otherwise I would tip it all away. Or throw it in my black hooded captor's face.

And there's the other problem. Who is my captor? I sense a familiarity and the navy-blue boilersuit clad figure holds just enough curve to mark her as woman. An aggressive woman who never speaks, just gestures me to keep away, in a far corner, waving a heavy metal pipe she carries in one hand. She then places a plastic bottle of drink and a large plastic mug of liquidised mush on the floor, just inside the door.

My head throbs, hunger twists my gut. A name hovers in my mind, but I can't grasp it or bring a face to the fore.

A woman. A man. Someone I know, but from where? Or is it someone I've just heard of but never met? Someone I'm still to meet. Just glimpses of memory, a mere glimmer of something before the darkness of now. Surely there must have been a before much different to this. When will I awake to it? When will it all come flooding back? Or will it stay lost forever? My brain aches with trying, as I pace like a caged tiger, but with no bars to see out onto whatever world I came from.

An unwelcome tiredness overtakes me as I slump in a corner and swig from my one luxury, the daily two-litre bottle of highly diluted fruit squash – peach tasting today, though barely so – not even sure who I really am. Or was.

Day 6

●●●

I've been asleep. I've no clue to what the time is, but it's not day. Darkness is complete. I'm trying to remember how long I've been here. At least four or five days. I can't be sure. I sense more than recount the meals and drinks I've been given, but not how many times there's been light creeping from the hatch. But that comes and goes even in short spells, disappearing when rain drums heavily on it before brightening again. But I have become more aware that that my present has a past. Hopefully a future, too.

My whole body aches from lying on cold concrete, sitting against damp chilled solid walls, forever circling these confines in slow steps. Slow steps. Slow steps. That triggers a memory. I used to run. I'm sure of it. And swim. But where? And with someone. That elusive name again, knocking on my temples. I have to focus. Patrick? Patricia? Am I being overtaken by insanity? Man or woman? Partner or friend? Brother or sister? My head screams.

Focus. If I ran, I must have done exercises. That's what I need to do now. That's what I can do now. Stretches, press-ups, squats and jump squats, plank, side plank, speed skaters, bird dogs, long jumps and more. They're crashing my memory with possibilities that don't need a gym. That won't make me giddy running around in circles. Fitness could help bring more memory back. It's coming to me. That's why I ran. To take away the tension of worries. To think problems through. Not as a competitive sport.

Fitness and purpose. Exercising will break up my day, give me a reason to keep going, despite this hell hole keeping me in the dark. I don't need light to get stronger. And strength will give me a greater chance of overpowering my captor. Strength and surprise. She'll think me too weak on her vile gruel and rationed drink. And I'm beginning to recall my old regime. Though I'll have to skip anything with weights. I daren't use the bucket for fear of spills. That doesn't bare thinking about.

But I need to remember more. If only my name. If only where I came from and especially who brought me here.

Slowly, a glimmer of light comes from overhead, through the narrow gape in the hatch. It's the morning of another squalid day, stuck in near total darkness with only the company of that foul smelling bucket.

Then there's the chink of metal as the key goes into the lock. Maybe a padlock, it seems to bounce and it's a different click when the door is shut again, I remember. The door opens warily outwards, as always, a hand and a steel pipe appearing slightly in front of the figure silhouetted by low daylight behind it. The back away gesture of her other hand is given, and I weakly comply. For now, anyway. A small metal tray with food and drink gives a low screech, as it's edged forward with her foot, across the concrete. Hidden eyes under a hoodie, that I guess never leave me. She half turns and in the dim light that comes through the doorway, I see her reach down for a plastic carrier which she throws towards me. For the first time I hear her voice. Barely more than a harsh whisper, so I have little chance of recognising it.

'Change your clothes. Dirty ones in the bag, back by the door. You have five minutes of light.'

She backs out, closes the door and the light comes on. My eyes sting with the sudden glare and keeping them half closed I rummage in the bag to find old but clean jeans, pants, but no bra and a scratchy wool top in old lady beige. But anything's better than the filthy, smelly, garments I'm wearing, so I hastily change, the light going out with the jeans half on.

The door opens.

'Bag.'

I throw it at the shadowy figure, it glances of her arm and lands on the tray, knocking over the drink, but just missing the gruel. She reaches down and pulls it though the doorway and I hear the click of the padlock. Yes, I'm sure it is a padlock, locking me in. So, I have a mushy soup, but no drink to sustain me until she collects the tray in some hours' time and replaces my empty bottle of squash with a fresh one.

But that voice stirred a memory. A voice of authority. A voice of aggression. A familiarity I can't quite place. Someone I know. Someone who hates me. Always has.

Day 7

●●●

The exercises I tried yesterday tired me quickly. I felt nauseous from each effort. But I now recognise the routine of each day. A mug of some thick drink in the morning, early, some nutritional beverage at a guess. Hours later is my meal. I laugh to myself at describing it as such. The lumpy broth has little taste, just some boiled up meat scraps and veg, heavy on hard potato lumps. But at least it keeps me alive. In the evening, the two-litre bottle of pale fruit squash. And in the middle of each night the light is switched on for about a minute or so. To purposely wake me or to see if I'm still alive? I don't know which.

I'm being a little gentler with my exercise this morning. Anger drove me to strive too hard yesterday, but my few sporadic hours of troubled sleep has changed my attitude. If I am to leave here, I've not just the problem of solving how. I need to know who I am and who my captor is, or I'll enter a strange world where I will be lost as what to do. I'll know no one to ask and, because everything is so quiet beyond the hatch, most of the time, I could find myself in an unpopulated wilderness, directionless, without anything to sustain me should I venture to find some form of local civilisation. A house, a farm, a village, a town.

I look up at the hatch. That sliver of inviting light that creeps through. I listen intently. Faintly, I hear sparrows squabbling nearby. And a gently rumbling hum from some distant road. Maybe a motorway, it seems so consistent. Wherever I am, it must be quite isolated. I realise I've only heard a few vehicle sounds close too. My captor coming and going, most likely. There must be other buildings, if this is a coal store of industrial size. Empty buildings, perhaps; or does she live here, this woman who radiates hate?

The door where she appears is a wide one. Was this once a factory? The other side, I think, would have been a boiler room. And above me a hard standing with the inset hatch I cannot reach. I cannot see through. I cannot unbolt. But there must be a way to reach it if the bolts are on the inside. I'll look again when the light comes on, tonight.

I've just done a few squats and a speed skater and it's refreshed me. My mind seems a little clearer. If I can remember these exercises, then I can remember more. I ask myself questions in my head. That name comes back. more clearly, now. Patricia. But is that me? I don't feel like a Patricia. I feel more like a … an Anna. I'm Anna! I know it. Relief floods through me as I remember my name. Anna Jane … Anna Jane and something else. Oh, come back to me. Anna Jane … Smithson.

I know who I am! But not the what's, why's and wherefores that go with that name. But a name is a start. If only I could write things down, so I don't lose the memory of them again. Will I remember my name tomorrow? That will be the real test. And who is Patricia? I need to tease more from my memory, but not now. My brain feels fuzzy. I must lie down. A sip of my drink and I'm spark out in moments.

I wake up at the sound of the padlock jostling, grab my squash and gulp down the last couple of inches in the bottle, warm and barely palatable. I would have normally finished it an hour or so ago. As her hoodie clad face appears around the door, I hold up the empty bottle.

'Bring.'

I walk calmly over, showing no intent of attacking her, and place the bottle down. She switches it for the filled one, a red colour tonight, steps back a pace and starts to shut the outward opening door.

'Thank you, Patricia,' I say, without thinking.

Her head jerks back, momentarily and for the first time I see her full face and the hatred in her cold eyes. She slams the door. Clicks the padlock. And I am wondering if I've given something away I should have kept secret. That I am regaining some memory.

Will that make matters worse for me?

I couldn't see the colour of her eyes, but I remember them clearly. Icy blue-grey. I just have to remember why.

Day 8

●●●

It must be a week. My incarceration. I remember, now being hurled through the door by strong arms, falling to the floor and, though barely conscious, hearing a ringing in my ears. Like faint but distinct notes. I heard them again this morning. The faint sound of distant church bells. It must be a Sunday. It's too early for a Saturday wedding. Knowing that, I feel less disoriented and gain a better sense of time.

Yesterday was the first real breakthrough of my memory. But from then on it went downhill. The foul gruel upset me. After a short session of floor exercises, the pain hit me in the gut, like a vicious punch. I spent most of the next few hours crouched over the bucket in the corner, arms and hands pressed against the walls for support, sweat pouring from my hot flushed face, fearful it would overflow and spread around my feet. Not that I have enough inside me to ever do that on the meagre rations I'm fed. I gag now on the mephitic odour, but daren't turn around to vomit.

There followed an exhaustion fuelled sleep. I didn't even wake to exchange my drinks bottle, but discovered it full, by my side, when wakened by the light flashing on for its minute's burn in the night.

This morning my head reels with a tight band of pain, my eyes sting and my legs feel jellified. I slump against the wall opposite the door and wait for that first clink and click which will herald the mug of some lukewarm, home concocted, not-so-smoothie.

I push back my shoulders and arch my back slightly to ease the nagging ache at the base and yesterday's bucket episode comes back to me. Although I seemed to have become oblivious to the stench in the room, a wave of nausea hits me. And a memory. The day I arrived here. Not all of it. Just the end.

I remembered being dragged down some dark steps, in some drunken state, and a door, or was it two, being pulled open and me being thrust into this filthy coal hole. The light came on and I was hauled up and sat against the wall. There were muttered words, something sarcastic, or maybe sadistic, like "Welcome to your new home," and "Over there's your luxury bathroom," with a hand pointing to the bucket in the corner, and an old tabloid newspaper next to it, which was obviously not for reading.

Then, when the light went out and my captor had gone, I tried to stand and feel around the walls, but slumped back down after just a few steps. I sat where I landed, tears on my cheeks, and tried to make out what had gone on in the hours before. I could recall nothing more than a few minutes ago and soon drifted into oblivion, to be woken up sometime later by a figure in a hoodie shaking my shoulder. My first thought was that Old Father Time had come to collect me, but I could see no scythe.

I was given a mug of hot drink, porridge thick, and I felt a sharp prick in my arm. I wore no outdoor clothes, just a light top and jeans and I was shivering with the cold. The warmth of the mug clasped in my two hands was the only element of bliss. And that was soon taken away. I fell into a troubled sleep, dreaming of big black birds, – crows, rooks, maybe – constantly flying around my head, cawing and wing-flapping, black beads of eyes staring at me, shooing me one way, then another until I felt the whole of my body spinning, falling, ever falling, into the unknown depths of a black walled chasm. The dream must have ended, but I can't recall how.

It's daytime now. The brightness at the hatch suggests the sun is shining. Suddenly, and unusually for the morning the light switches on. I look up at the hatch while I can see it properly, conscious that the door will open any minute. And it does, but regrettably I have had time to see that what I thought were bolts, which I'd tried so unsuccessfully to reach, were merely strips of reinforcement to the opening edges. The hatch, like the door, can only be opened outwards.

Then she appears. This time the hood around her shoulders, and I can see her fiery red cropped hair and fierce ice-clear stare. A face instantly recognised. Not Patricia. Patrycja. Polish. Means noble. Not this Patrycja, though. Not by birth nor demeanour.

We stay silent a moment, staring into each other's depths. She calculating. Me wondering. How much can I remember? Why has she done this? Who will make the next move?

The slap across my face comes from nowhere. I stagger, but I'm determined not to fall. Mouth pinched shut, I stay silent. Make her speak first, I think, do not plead, stand tall. If I don't move, I have the advantage. I've had plenty of practice keeping silent in this dark pit.

'You think you remember me. But do you really know me?' Her words come out harsh and dry, unwavering eyes boring into mine. 'And what other memories have you been dwelling on, with all this time to yourself?'

It's only now I realise she is unarmed with her usual iron bar. Not that I would risk attacking her. I'm not yet back to any degree of strength. And she obviously knows it. Neither do I have any weapon other than an empty plastic bottle. There is the bucket of putrid excrement, but that's too far away to reach without an obvious move. The bucket that is emptied only every two days and which she takes out without fuss, seeming oblivious to the nauseating odour. I want to look around for a means of escape, but I am hypnotised by her penetrating fix on my eyes, as if trying to see into my very soul. I may not have regained much physical strength, but I have a stubborn mind at the best of times, and driven by my current extreme, I remain unblinking, facing her down with resolve.

'You may have realised my name,' Patrycja continues after minutes of silence, 'but how much else do you recall? It would be unusual for you to recover much of your memory, devoid of all prompts. Perhaps your own name? But not how you came to be here? I hazard a guess the blankness of your mind is just a mirror of the blackness of this cell. And so it shall remain, for as long as I choose.

'Now stand back against the wall, feet apart, arms straight out sideways, palms against it.'

I step back, meekly, not sure what I can do to resist. I could try to make a dash for the door, but I'm not yet ready, yet, to find out what will happen if I fail to reach it.

'Good girl. Stay that way until I've gone, and you will get your usual fare for today. Cross me and it will be withdrawn, and you will know the pain of real hunger before you are fed again. You, my girl, have taken a vow of silence, though maybe not of your own choosing. No one knows where you are. And they've no reason to think you are missing. I've made sure of that, for the time being. No one is looking for you. So, I'll leave you to your memories, what little they might be, for that's what they will stay. Just memories.'

Spreadeagled against the wall even the tiniest of movement will alert her to any aggression from me, so she calmly removes my drinks bottle and the bucket, leaves, and closes the door behind her. I now must wait for her next food visit. She left me no breakfast mug and she's taken the dregs of my drink. But the light is still on. A change of tactics I guess, to disturb my mind, to confuse my memory. I now know for sure who my captor is, but I can't think why she is.

Day 9

●●●

I think this is worse than the dark. The light has stayed on ever since early yesterday, after Patrycja's warning visit. My gruel came as usual, and so did my fruit squash, both delivered in silence. Not that the light is very bright. Most of it is absorbed by the grimy grey walls. It disturbed my sleep, disoriented me, and somehow makes the space seem even smaller, even more crowding, makes my head spin even more with the effort of drawing back memories. And with that dreaded bucket always in view it magnifies its foulness, constantly reminding me of the disgusting conditions in which I'm imprisoned.

One thing, though, it did give me a chance to thoroughly inspect this hellhole and see that there is absolutely no way of getting out except through the single door. The coal hatch I can't reach, and it's never opened any way. I did manage to peer around Patrycja as she brought in this morning's breakfast mug. Just enough to see another door on the far wall of the adjacent room, short brick pillars which probably once supported a boiler and a splash of light on the floor that looked as if it came from a barred roof light, highlighting a swirl of dust motes disturbed by her passage. How come I can recognise these details easily, yet I can't remember anything about me? But the most important detail was the loose brick or two I spotted on the floor. One of those could be useful if I can get past my captor.

The revelation of my captor had shocked all other thoughts out of my mind yesterday, as I gathered the bare threads of who she was and how I knew her. We had worked in the same office at some time past, and I recalled her being an efficient, if slightly officious, colleague who was a strict disciplinarian of a team leader. She commanded respect despite a low level of rankling within her team, all of whom were totally loyal to her should any negative remark be made from outsiders.

Patrycja had a disarming smile whenever she wanted to display it, but much of the time she dealt her cards with little emotion. She was a business machine with an inventive brain who knew what she wanted, where she was going and would accept no resistance to her upward career climb. I envied her drive and thought her a good role model by which to set my own standards. Except my brain never worked like hers. Not as fast, nor as visionary as she appeared to be. When she was promoted above me, I accepted she deserved it, I remember that, but what we did and in what office is still too fuzzy to recall. I can visualise two rows of workstations and some glass panelled offices along the side. What did I actually do as a job? And where? Was I at one of the workstations or in a side office? Was it in finance, marketing, sales management? I'm sure I, too, was responsible for a team. But I can't recall any names or faces.

Today, I've completely lost track of time again. With the light on, the glimmer from the ill-fitting hatch doors, above, hardly competes. It could be early morning, early evening, or the middle of a dull day. My odd snatches of sleep have upset any pattern and the only clue has been the breakfast mug of some cereal drink, which seems hours ago. I suppose that rules out early morning, at least. Thankfully my bowels are more settled now, and I can exercise again without risk of a sudden explosion from my gut. I sit in the corner furthest away from the bucket in a vague yoga pose and try to meditate. Not that I've ever practised yoga, as far as I know. I just need to clear confusing thoughts out of my mind and try to remember more about me than just my name. Just who was … is … Anna Jane Smithson?

I must have drifted off, again. I didn't hear the click of the padlock, but I was suddenly aware of the door being open and Patrycja sliding in the tray with today's meal. Not the usual gruel but sandwiches and an apple. I blinked the sleep out of my eyes, and despite my low state, sarcasm got the better of me.

'We having a party? Something to celebrate?'

She didn't reply, straightaway, but placed two bottles of fruit squash alongside the tray together with two unopened plastic packs of sandwiches and a pack of breakfast biscuits.

'Sorry, there's no champagne,' she said without a smile and with a level, no nonsense, tone. 'You'll be partying on your own for the next two days. Don't make a pig of yourself, expecting more tomorrow. It won't come.'

No chance of that, the diet she is keeping me on. It's probably a good thing there's no mirror down here. I hate to think what a wrinkled old wreck I must be coming. Perhaps I can rush her, now, while she thinks I'm weak and sleepy and get through the doorway. But as soon as I move to get up from the floor, she steps back and slams the door. This time I do here the click of the padlock.

So, thwarted before I was even on my feet, I settle back to two days of total isolation. Two days in light bright enough to disturb my sleep and add to my confusion of time, no doubt. Just a little to eat and plenty to think about. Including how to escape.

Day 10

●●●

The breakfast biscuits I ate this morning were far better than the thick smoothies and cereal drinks I've had so far, but I could do with more drink than the two large bottles I'm eking out. At least the pail won't overflow while I'm waiting for Patrycja to make her next appearance. I'm in the dark again. The light went out quite soon after her last visit. Complete dark. Something has been moved over the hatch, so there's not even a glimmer from up there.

On the bright side I've figured out my way to escape and feel my exercising has built up enough energy for that. I've pulled up some more memories, too, so I'm beginning to get a picture of who I am and why I'm here. Still a bit sketchy. But beginning to make sense.

I have an image of a flat in a city, small but modern. Quite minimalist décor and furnishings. Is that by design or lack of money? I can't say. I can't remember anyone else living there. No flatmate, no partner, no pet. I know it's in a city because outside the window I just see buildings, close packed, Edwardian frontages on my street, but tall office like buildings further away. Perhaps I work in one of them. I sense an aroma of coffee. I drink a lot of coffee, freshly ground in a bean-to-cup machine. Impress my friends with my barista skills. Oh, that I could have one now. A simple latté or, better still, a warming mocha. But I'm torturing myself thinking about it. And the friends that appear in my mind are nameless faces I don't yet recognise.

If I can just get through this day, tomorrow I can break out. Get back to the real world. As long as my escape plan works. It must. I have to remain positive.

Another memory that has come to the surface is my job. I'm middle management in an insurance company, dealing with housing claims from developers. Problems with new and recent builds that are in dispute with both sub-contractors and property buyers, some domestic but mostly commercial on my remit. I have a team of four who report to me and there's another team headed up by Patrycja that outperforms everyone on the floor. She's due for promotion if I remember right. Or has she already moved upstairs as an associate director? I can't make up my mind. I know she deserves it. She's saved the company a fortune in case dismissals, finding oblique interpretations of cover that put more onus on the insured than they had realised. They may read the small print, she used to say, but they rarely understand all the ifs and buts the words envelope. I know she was always very clever in her wording: strictly legal terminology, but the full meaning not always obvious to the untrained eye. Stuart is always praising her.

That's the final clue. Stuart. I know it. But why. Stuart, Stuart. Why can't I remember Stuart other than just a name? I know he's important in this, but why? Stuart … Stuart Bembrige. Soft Scot's accent. A director where I work. Blue eyes. Dark wavy hair. Drives a red Porsche Cayenne Coupé. I've been in it. But when? And why?

My heads in a tight ring of subdued pain, like a huge rubber band relentlessly compressing it. I need to remember more. Patrycja, Stuart and me. Is there a common factor, other than where we work? Something we do or share? Why do I get such disjointed flashes of recall?

I'm thirty-two. Where's that come from, I wasn't even thinking about me? I was trying to focus on Stuart. He's thirty-five. A good six inches taller than me, athletic, has a dark blue tracksuit with white stripes. Adidas. I can picture him running alongside me. Was that by chance or did we plan it? Nothing more comes.

Hunger is taking precedence now. I've put off opening one of the extra sandwiches for as long as possible. I don't know whether Patrycja will be back tonight or tomorrow. All else I've got until she does, is my carefully rationed squash. It's difficult to plan when I don't know the actual time or how long since my last bite or drink. And boredom drives into patchy snatches of sleep, without regard to any clock. I feel drowsy, now. Time for some floor exercises to tone up my body and liven my mind.

Day 11 – Morning

● ● ●

What I take to be night came and went with no sign of Patrycja. Yet the light came on for a short spell as it has before. Is she, or someone else spying on me? During the time the light was left on constantly, I examined every inch of wall I could see and all around the single door. I could see no sign of any electronic device that could record or view me. I'm positive the short spell of light is just to disturb me. To keep my brain confused. It seems to be working, anyway.

This morning, however, I feel a little more alive. It might be the exercises taking effect or, maybe, the different food. If, as I suspect, I have been drugged previously, there was unlikely to be anything in the fare out of sealed packets.

There's that rattle and click at the door again. She's back, opening the padlock. Too, soon to make my escape, but time to make the first move towards it. I hurry to the back wall and lean with my head pressed against it and wait. The light goes on. The door is drawn back, and I sense the figure of Patrycja staring across at me. I hear the clunk of the breakfast mug being set down on the floor. And slow, wary paces towards me.

'No funny games, please. Turn around and face me.' Her voice is stern. The same voice I used to hear in the office when she called a member of her team to order, usually for perceived under achievement.

I stay stock still.

'Anna! No time for silly games. You know you'll never get the better of me. You're too weak. In body and in mind.' She used my name. Has she guessed I've remembered it, or has she made her first slip?

As she venomously spits the last few words, I half turn to see she is staying well back, obviously ready to grab me if I try to run.

'It's not a game,' I say weakly, looking back at her with half closed eyes. 'I feel so faint and woozy, and my head is pounding. Can I have some painkillers, or something? Please.'

'That's just your change of diet for a couple of days. You'll be back to your usual routine now I'm back.' She sounds totally unsympathetic. 'Pick up your rubbish and bottles and place them by the door.' She sidles quickly back to block the doorway and any attempt by me to escape.

I gather up the empty sandwich and biscuit packets, the bottles, and the tray, and move to the door, painfully slowly, feeling her eyes fixed on me the whole time. I place them at her feet and look directly at her, my brow furrowed, and eyes half closed in apparent pain. I'm tempted to charge into her, but now's not the time. So, I turn away and walk back to the far wall and wait until I hear the door click shut, before I slowly cross back to pick up my mug of breakfast sludge.

The wait for my next tray meal, the highlight of each day, is going to be a long one, I'm sure. Or will certainly seem so. For only then can I put my plan into full action.

But, a total surprise, within twenty minutes or half-hour, at a guess, the padlock clicks, and the door opens a crack. Patrycja slides through a litre bottle of water and two blue and white capsules cut from a blister pack. Probably, paracetamol.

'You're probably just dehydrated,' she says, and shuts the door before I have time to say thanks, which I might not have done, anyway.

I pop the capsules out and drop them into the bucket, fouler than ever, not being changed yesterday. No way am I going to risk taking them, however innocuous they might look, even though my head does really throb for much of the time. The water is welcome, though, after I've checked the seal hasn't been broken.

It's slightly chilled. She must have a fridge somewhere near or just come back from a shop. There must be some civilisation close by if the latter. Somewhere I can get to quickly when I escape. And today I will. I'm all set. It's going to be a strain, but I mustn't doze off, so I'll keep exercising. I have to be alert when I hear the padlock clink.

I'm remembering more, while I wait. I was out in some gentle green hills, a country park, on one of my regular runs across well-used footpaths, when I heard a kissing gate I'd just passed through click shut. I glanced behind to see another lone figure behind me. I wasn't far into my run and my competitive instinct was to increase my pace, but I could hear footsteps gaining on me. I stumbled, tried to right myself, then in the next couple of paces turned my ankle over on a loose stone. As I was falling, I felt a strong hand grip my arm to break my fall, at first closing my eyes in embarrassment at ending up on the ground. After a moment of catching my breath, I looked up, to say thankyou and saw it was Stuart. I now felt even more embarrassed. He knelt down and felt my ankle, sprained but not broken, he thought, and lifted me carefully to my feet. Brooking no argument, he supported me as I hobbled back to the pub car park where he started the run and steered me over to his car. That's how I know how swish it was.

He asked me where my car was, and I told him I'd jogged the first three-quarters of a mile from the edge of town, where I lived, to warm up. He offered to take me to the hospital, but I said no, I could walk the pain off, for the rest of the way, but he wouldn't hear of that. So, he gave me a lift home. He found my coffee machine and made both of us a mocha. He found a pack of frozen broad beans and laid that over my ankle, after he made me sit on the sofa with my foot up. I remember he stayed a long time. I remember he was most attentive. I remember him making me breakfast.

My mind makes me wonder if it was purely by chance he was running behind me, that day. We'd talked quite casually in the office a few times about what we did away from work. Just polite chit-chat, I thought at the time, even though I was drawn to him more than any other current male friend. And I had told him where my favourite runs were.

I also remember Patrycja telling me she had her sights on him and I knew that what Patrycja wants she usually gets. By fair means? Not always.

Day 11 – Afternoon

•••

It seems a longer wait than usual between breakfast and my stingy main meal. But as soon as I hear the click of the padlock being removed, I tip the bucket over quietly and drop face down next to, but not quite in, the flood of excrement. Eyes gently closed, as if unconscious, and trying not to gag on the foul stench, I wait those long seconds before the light comes on and Patrycja opens the door. I can feel her cold eyes boring into me as she must be taking in the scene.

'Anna! No silly games. Get up.'

Naturally she expects some ruse, but this time patience is going to be my reward. I stay still and silent.

'Don't try to fool me. Anna, what's wrong with you?' She sounds exasperated, but I am gambling on having sown the seed of really being unwell earlier today. It's a struggle to stay prone, I want to get away from the mess next to me before I really pass out. I remain painfully still, on the cold concrete floor and hear her steps as she approaches, slowly, to look closer.

Her hand takes my wrist to find a pulse. I keep my breathing slow and quiet. She takes my shoulders gently and starts to turn me over. I give the barest quiver of my eyes, slitting them enough to see, as I guessed, that she has dropped down on her haunches to examine me. I explode into action pushing myself up, flailing my arms and legs to see her topple over inelegantly sideways, and I make a run for the door, but slip in the greasy mess I spilled, tumbling forward onto my hands. I push myself up and forwards quickly knowing I could still be through the door before she was half up, with time to slam it shut and drop the padlock into the hasp.

Except there is no padlock. She must have it in a pocket of the hoodie she always wears, probably wary of an action like I just made, and to be sure she couldn't be locked in. I spin on my heel and race for the far door, hoping it will lead to stairs and the outside world. I pull it, I push it, it won't budge It's locked. Patrycja is obviously a very cautious lady.

Turning I see her striding towards me, and I dive to my right to pick up a large piece of brick from the floor, holding it high, ready to use as a weapon. But she just stops and smiles.

'You never did think far enough ahead, Anna. That's why you've never made it upstairs, where I am now. In an office right next to Stuart. Put the brick down. You haven't the strength to use it. There is no escape unless I decide where you next go. And not all escapes are pleasant. Unless, perhaps, you might find eternal darkness rewarding.'

I throw the brick at her, missing her by a foot as she dodges sideways and launches herself towards me ready to grab my arm. As the weight of her much stronger body is about to hit me, I just go limp and sink downwards and the force of her charge takes us both to the floor, but she loses any grip and a quick push with my hand against the concrete rolls us both over so that I end up on top. I clasp her neck in a strangle hold, but I am not strong enough to stop her wrenching them away, bucking her body so that I slide off her and she, once again has the advantage. I look for a more manageable half-brick, spot one close by, and as I roll over and reach out for it, Patrycja springs back up, like a cat, and steps down hard on the back of my wrist. The pain sears up my forearm.

Now flat on the floor, face down, casting my eyes left and right, I spot a short length of steel pipe propped against the wall, by the door into my coal cellar cell, the one she used at first to make me to back away from her. If only I can get to that, somehow – before she remembers it.

'That's enough you stupid bitch! Don't think I haven't made sure there's no way you can leave unless I choose. And at the moment there's no chance of that. You're going to serve your time until my wishes are complete. When you next see the light of day, no one will believe any story you tell. You'll have lied to your friends, betrayed the man you say you love, and you will have been summarily dismissed from your job for taking leave without notice, during an important policy negotiation. Typical failure of someone who can't cope, they'll say. You're the one who will appear to be vindictively desperate. A loser trying to pass blame onto anyone but yourself. Especially when your befuddled memory can't explain how you got here or even exactly where this is.'

I find my voice, despite the pressure of her knee on my back. 'Whatever lies you make up, the truth will come out. I can't just disappear without some ripples already. No texts, no Facebook or Twitter, no phone calls. That's not like me. Suspicion will already be roused. You'll never get away with this.'

'On the contrary, my darling Anna. I have your phone and access to your laptop. You really should choose stronger passwords, not that my friend in IT couldn't break them. Silly man thinks he's on a promise, as well as a little cash bonus.' Patrycja has become almost gleeful. 'You've sent plenty of texts and tweets, your Facebook page is up to date, and you've made some lovely comments about your friend Sue's new baby. And you've uploaded some beautiful pictures of your adventure in Thailand, that someone so unexpectedly offered you. Such short notice though, but a chance you just couldn't miss. And knowing the firm wouldn't give you six weeks leave of absence, you just upped and quit. Wasn't I kind to plead your case to HR, saying you'd been very stressed lately and must be having some sort of mental breakdown? Not that it did much good.'

'If this is Thailand where's the sun?' is all I could retort, as I let her ease me off the floor and lead me back towards my prison. As I relax my body in submission, so does she loosen her grip slightly, more intent on steering me than being over physical. I expect to get a hefty push in the back though, once we reach the doorway. But it's not the doorway I keep my eye on. Just as we draw level, I jerk myself sideways and grab the length of pipe propped there, with my free hand, and swing it back over my head onto hers. I hear the crack of steel on bone, and she drops to the floor in a heap.

No time to lose. No time to check her health, as I feel around her pockets for keys. Finding the padlock first, I'm tempted to roll her into the coal store and see how she fares on a day in the dark, but she looks as though she'll be in the dark, anyway, long enough for me to escape. In another pocket I find four keys on a split ring. I take them and run back to the far door, trying them one by one, third time lucky. There are stairs to my right, leading to a solid dark red door with a broad metal kick plate at the base. Will that be locked, too?

Day 12

●●●

I'm lost. Totally lost. I've had no food or drink since yesterday. I'm weak and tired, with just a couple of hours of troubled, cold, outdoor sleep. And I'm worried about Patrycja. Did I hit her too hard? Is she still lying on that concrete floor, disabled, unconscious, or worse? Should I go back, to see.

I acted too hastily, yesterday. The thought of freedom outweighed any other measures and I just wanted to get away as far as I could before finding help. The door at the top of the stairs was unlocked and led into a high roofed industrial building, long abandoned judging by the general emptiness and spread of pigeon droppings. I could hear them cooing in the rafters and I jumped with a start, flinching, when one flew in through an open window that hung at an odd angle from its hinges. But there was a door just along from it, and after finding which of the keys fitted the lock, that was my way out onto a hardstanding where a red Land Rover Discovery Sport was parked, half hidden from outside view by an old industrial dumpster. Patrycja's car. The perfect means of escape – if I only had the key. I ran over and took a quick look, hoping, but not believing, she might have left the key in the ignition and immediately saw it was a keyless model. I could have gone down to search her pockets, but the risk was too great. If she had recovered, she might expect me to do that and lie in wait. Best I disappeared, fast.

There was no nearby housing or immediately apparent road, just a rutted driveway running across farmland. The road would be down there somewhere, but I would be visible for a long way should Patrycja give chase. And she would just jump into her Discovery. Over to my left I could see mixed woodland that stretched up a low rise from the acres of flatland in front to me. I headed for that and met a high chain-link fence on its border. I turned and looked behind me. Still no sign of Patrycja, so I paced along the fence hoping for a gateway and found my first lucky break. An old beech tree had fallen across it pulling the top wires down leaving a vee shaped gap entangled with its branches. With just a little difficulty, I was able to hoist my way through by clambering over the stouter limbs. While I was raised from the ground I looked back at the emptiness and on the far side of the building from which I had escaped, I saw a row of old Nissen huts. It looked like the land had once been a wartime airfield, now returned to agriculture. Had I run the wrong way? Was there anyone in those huts, probably now used as lock-up business units?

Too late to turn back, I hurried on into the wood, without any thought to direction and after what seemed an age, but was probably less then half-an-hour, I sat down, my back against a tree trunk, and wept. I was free of my captivity, but how do I find someone to help me, when I know little more than my name, not even where I live and have a barely credible tale of being locked in a cellar for days? I can't even tell anyone where that cellar is. And who'll believe my social posts were faked once I find my home again?

After a brief rest, I walked further into the woodland, and once confident that Patrycja wouldn't venture so deep after me, I found a small clearing to settle down and rest. The light was going fast, but the darkness that settled was nowhere near as dark as that fearsome coal cellar. Throughout the night I jumped and stirred at the strange noises of the woodland, ears attuned to anything that sounded like footsteps, eyes searching for any movement in barely discernible surroundings, until eventually falling into a dream filled sleep, before waking to a dull and dismal dawn.

Now, I am trudging through trees, without any clue in what direction. There's no sun to guide me, nor features that stand out. Just tree after tree. I could be walking in circles, or deeper still towards the centre, the greyness above the canopy unrelentingly even. At least in that cell I knew where I was. I could find food and drink, even if the gruel was gruesome. Here I made do with a few cupped handfuls from a rainwater puddle. At least, I hope it was rainwater. It didn't taste too pure.

This is becoming more frightening than my days in the dark. There's no one to help me, no one to guide me, or provide food, and the few berries I've seen look poisonously red. I'm no nature girl for all my love of the wild.

What's that? I hear a sharp crack behind me, though not very loud. Is somebody following me? I take a couple more paces forward and slowly turn around, scanning in every direction. I see nothing other than trees and a few bushes. And two grey squirrels chasing up a tree trunk. I've now lost all sense of the direction I was going. I move on – forwards, backwards, sideways, to where I'd set my path, I can't say. I peer around for signs of any brightening and my eyes alight on a definite track in the undergrowth. Animal probably, but I follow it, eyes to the ground tracing the way ahead. A sudden loud crashing and fluttering breaks my concentration, makes my heart momentarily leap with fear, as two wood pigeons take flight on my approach. It makes me look sideways and a short way to my right I notice a dark line running between the ferns and brushwood. I pace over to see and discover a cinder path.

I sigh with relief. This is a path that will take me somewhere. I might even find someone walking it. But which way is safest to go? Choose wrong and I could end up back near where I was held captive. That might be dangerous, certainly not helpful. Looking both ways I sense, rather than see, a slight lightening in the trees and head that way, around two curves and then a sharp bend in the path, all the time wondering if my strength will hold out to carry me much farther. Then I spot it. Tiny looking from a distance but bringing hope: a metal gate onto a road. I know it's a road. I've just seen and heard a blue van and a silver car flash past, seconds apart.

With renewed energy I jog down to the gate and step out onto a grass verge. Not a vehicle in sight. It's not a busy road, it's a narrow lane. Which way to go is obvious, though. Downhill. The other way curves up into a steep rise and I haven't the energy for that. I cross over to the right-hand side and plod wearily onwards, and after a few minutes I hear something approaching behind me. I turn and wave my hand to flag it down so I can at least ask where I am. It's a small saloon with a middle-aged couple in the front seats. And it slows right down as it sees me. Then accelerates past. I shouldn't be surprised; I must look a bedraggled wreck.

I get the same treatment three more times, so I decide to just drag myself on until I find a house or farm or any other form of habitation, but I really need a few minutes break before I do. There's a field gate on my side of the road and I slump down with my back against it. I lower my head into my hands, rubbing my eyes and pass into a semi-sleep as I try to think where I could possibly be. And it's in this dreamy state I hear this young lad's voice.

'Yer OK, missus? I need to fetch the cows through.'

Day 13

●●●

I wake up in a hospital bed. It's a private room – another cell. All pastels, white and clean. And I have a drip leading to the cannula in my left arm. There's a nurse with her back to me tapping something onto her iPad, or whatever tablet she's got. She turns around and I flinch. She has the same colour eyes and hairstyle as Patrycja, and I see her pick up a syringe from the table at the end of the bed. But her eyes sparkle as she smiles.

'You awake, then? You're a lucky girl. If that farm lad hadn't found you, you'd be in here with hypothermia. As it is, all you really needed was a little warming up, re-hydration and a good long sleep. Are you feeling better for that?

I don't really know how I feel, so I just nod a vague yes.

'Now when you came in you were very weak so couldn't tell us much. We think you said your name was Ann or Anna something so Ann's the name above your bed. Is that right?'

'Anna,' I reply in a drowsy voice. I still feel exhausted. 'Anna Jane Smithson.' I marvel that the memory comes straight to me.

'That's fine. I'll just add an 'a' and we can fill in the rest of your details in a few moments.' She leans over and corrects the whiteboard above my head with a black marker, then takes the notes from the end of my bed and writes in my full name. 'Doctor Kensington should be around to see you in about twenty minutes. But first let's get you some breakfast. I had brought you in a fortifying drink, but that's gone cold. I am sure we can do better. I'll help you sit up.' She unhooks the bed control and raises the back, then comes and adjusts both me and the pillows. On the over-bed table I can see the mug of gruel and start to retch.

'Not that drink please, but can I just have some water, for now.'

'Sure you don't want tea or coffee?'

'Not just for the moment, thank you.' Memories are flooding into my mind. Dark memories.

But not just the dark ones. During my time in that disorienting woodland, I had plenty of time to think, without disturbance from Patrycja, without any mind-numbing additions to my meagre rations and realised why she had taken against me so vilely. The traits I had admired her for, the determination and drive that had led to her success in business also belied a vicious streak that had no conscience when achieving her aims. The strict rule of her team should have given that away, the misplaced loyalty built on fear rather than trust. It all became so clear.

She had mapped out exactly how to get to the top and was on the penultimate rung of the ladder, with her promotions, needing just one more ally to hold close to her; emotionally close to her. And I'd inadvertently secured that prize. Stuart. I had to be removed from the scheme, discredited, shown to be unreliable, disloyal and have no regard for job, my clients, or my colleagues. At least she'd stopped short of murder – so far. But what had been her end game intention? She could hardly let me come back into the company and cause consternation from any accusations I made. I had to be away for long enough to be deemed a total liar and cheat with an unfounded grudge against her. That's if I was ever allowed to return at all. I have a strong feeling I would have been despatched too long and too far, for that to happen. The coal cellar would not have been my final resting place. For some reason she needed to keep me alive. Perhaps, if she didn't get her final wish, she could use me as some bargaining chip with Stuart, who she would no doubt oust once his immediate usefulness had expired. Might even reunite us if we agreed to remove ourselves from the scene. It's all just conjecture because nothing else makes sense.

But most importantly I have recalled who I am, that Stuart and I had announced our engagement and planned a celebration with colleagues and friends and my last memory is of two days before the planned night and Patrycja inviting me around to her apartment for a drink, telling me not to say anything to Stuart because she was planning a little surprise for him. I went there straight from work. That must have been the night I disappeared. The night my drink was spiked. The night I was thrown into the cellar. The night she must have relieved me of my phone and my laptop. But did she take my car as well and hide it somewhere?

The nurse and the doctor are back. And another woman. A detective, I wonder, hopefully. But no, she is a psychiatrist. It says so on her badge.

'You look much better, Anna. I'm Doctor Kensington. Paul Kensington. And this is Laura Cole, who has come to help me assess you now that you are recovering. I don't know how much you remember of arriving here yesterday, but you were suffering from severe exhaustion and close to hypothermia. You were certainly not dressed for a night out in the woods, as you say you had been. In fact, it was quite a tale you reeled off to us, but you seemed barely conscious while you told it. I think there might have been some confusion in your mind, which is quite understandable, considering the state you were in.'

'So, let me give you a quick health check and we can remove the drip line. Then Laura, here, will listen to your story. Nurse Barratt will run over your personal details, and you can tell us who we need to inform that you're here. Or you can phone them yourself if you feel strong enough and prefer that.'

I can hardly remember arriving here, let alone what I said. If it was about my imprisonment, escape, and night in the woods, they must think I'm a raving loony. I wouldn't believe it if I didn't know it was true. Hence the presence of Laura Cole, I suppose. Thankfully the doctor is quick, gives a smile of satisfaction and looks as if he's going to give me a pat on the head, like I've been a good little girl. Instead, he just asks the nurse to remove the drip and cannula, saying to me. You seem fine, but you could do with a little more weight on you. Are you worried about your weight, and have you been on a slimming diet?'

He thinks I might have an eating disorder, now, another reason for his colleague's presence. He's right in one way, but it's not been through my own choice. I reply 'Not intentionally. I usually keep myself fit with a good diet and plenty of exercise. That just hasn't been possible lately. Once I leave here, I'll get back to that.'

'Fine. Generally, there seems little to worry about, physically, but I'm going to keep you in another day for observation and then if my colleague is happy, we can let you go home.' He nods towards Dr Cole and walks out of my room and hands the folder of my notes to Nurse Barratt, who goes through my name, address, next of kin and the like. I'm surprised that I remember it all, but it's quickly done.

The nurse passes the notes folder over to Dr Cole, who glances through them and then says, 'You seem to have had a really bad experience, Anna. It is alright for me to call you Anna, isn't it?' She doesn't wait for a reply but sees me nod yes. 'You can call me Laura and we can forget any doctor stuff. Take your own time and I know it's traumatic but try to tell me how you feel and how you came to be here.'

Just the two of us left in the room, now, and a chance to set out my plight. I just hope I'm believed.

Day 14 – Morning

●●●

I can't tell you how much better it is to wake up normally, well almost normally, to daylight and sunshine. I feel a weight of worry lifting of me, and I've had time to review the events of yesterday. The doctor, the psychiatrist – and the policeman.

I've enjoyed a hospital breakfast without a hint of gruel, with just a visit from Nurse Barratt, who now answers to Julie, and a junior nurse, Mahalia. They've both been really attentive and brought me up to date with what's been happening in the outside world over the last week or two. Not much different from the usual political squabbles and celebrity disputes, it seems. But it helps me ground myself as I work out what I need to do next.

During a long discourse with Laura Cole, in which I tried to relay the whole story of the last few days as concisely as possible, I wasn't surprised to see a police constable at the door. I asked him if they had found Patrycja and arrested her. I wanted to know if she was alright, but didn't want to ask directly, for obvious reasons. I'm not going to risk a charge of manslaughter, or worse, if she didn't make it, after my heavy blow to her head. It was self-defence, but how would I prove that. Anyway, he said he knew nothing about that and had been sent to ask a few questions about the incident in Tuppence Halfpenny Lane. How I had got there, where had I come from, was I a heavy drinker or on drugs, did I have any medical issues, physical or mental, what I was doing there, and was I a lookout for cattle rustlers. They'd had a few problems with the last, just lately. I couldn't believe it. At least I found out that the lad who'd come down on his bike to fetch the cows for milking had helped me away from the gate and phoned 999, while his herd of dairy cows had trundled out of the field and down the lane. They knew the way to go, with a little push or two from his dad, who had followed him down. But I'd passed out by then and never saw all that. I said I wanted to thank him, and the PC gave me his name, Cecil Trouton, and that I'd find him at Cranberry Farm. I also told him what had happened to me, prior to being found by Cecil, but he seemed to wave that away as if it was make believe.

Thinking back to how I got here from that gateway, I recall coming round on a gurney being trundled into A&E and have a hazy memory of being poked and prodded, lying half-awake for what seemed all day, in a long corridor, then being transferred to a bed and hooked up to a drip, no doubt sedated, as my next memory is waking up yesterday morning at nearly midday. I now must wait for Doctor Kensington, who should be on his ward round anytime soon.

Without the controlling drugs that Patrycja must have been adding to my food and drink, I can remember most things about my life, except a blank spot between her inviting me around to her place and waking up fuzzy and memoryless in that evil black hole. I feel fit, if still a little fatigued, and hope to be discharged once the doctor has seen me.

The door has just been opened by him, and the doctor and Nurse Barratt come and stand at the end of my bed. I'm sitting in a chair at the side, still in a hospital gown, hoping my clothes will be returned to me. They are not in the bedside locker.

'Good morning, Anna. I'm pleased to see you looking much brighter, this morning,' he says after a brief look at my medical notes. You've recovered surprisingly well from your trauma and all the signs show you should be fully fit in just a few days. However, we are keeping you here for another day to see some final test results, to ensure there's nothing insidious still lurking in your body. Nothing that might have caused your malnutrition or that could lead to another blackout.'

I'm thinking, I've told you what, or rather who, caused my malnutrition and sheer exhaustion caused the final blackout. What more do they need to know?

Nurse Barratt reads the disappointment (and disbelief) on my face. 'I'm sure you want to get back home all the sooner, but we must be sure that you are completely ready. We know about your recent memory losses and irrational behaviour. All we want is to be completely sure you leave here without any likelihood of a relapse. Laura Cole wants to see you again this afternoon. She will explain the options for further treatment, which she thinks you may need.'

'Treatment for what?' I feel annoyed by the insinuation I need psychiatric help. All I need is to see Patrycja brought to justice. And a few good meals inside me.

'Laura will explain,' Doctor Kensington continues. 'You have had an unnerving experience and in view of past episodes we just want to ensure you're in the best state of health, both physically and mentally.'

'And what do you mean by past episodes?' Am I missing something here? I've said nothing to imply I've any other issues. I haven't any.

Nurse Barratt, again. 'It's nothing to worry about. We had a talk with your sister Pat, who thought you were abroad on holiday. She seems very worried about you. She explained everything to us about before. Just talk to Laura Cole, this afternoon, and I'm sure you'll feel happier.'

'But I don't have a sister Pat. I'm an only child. What are you talking about?' I'm getting a little scared. Do they really think I'm a mental case? Do they even believe what I've told them?

'Yes, dear, your sister, did say you'd had a dissociative disorder once before, but she's coming in to visit you tomorrow morning to explain more. However, we may still allow you to go back home with her if Dr Cole thinks you're ready.'

I'm astounded. It doesn't take much working out that Pat is Patrycja and survived. She must have known I wouldn't get far and would likely end up in hospital, considering the fragile state she'd brought me to. Time to change tack and not react too fiercely, even though I could happily jump out of this chair and throttle both of them. 'Have the police been able to trace that person I told you about?'

It's the doctor's turn. 'We thought we'd wait until you were feeling better before we involve any police. We don't want to exhaust you with unnecessary questioning, but we have a record of what you told us.'

He must see the astonished look on my face because he quickly adds that he must complete his ward round and turns to go. He doesn't want to explain his actions. As he gets to the door, I suggest the police might like to come tomorrow, when my sister arrives and talk to me with her present, too. He gives a vague nod and a 'Hmph' and carries on out, closely followed by Nurse Barratt, who turns at the door and says in her matter-of-fact calm. 'She's bringing in some clothes for you tomorrow. In the meantime, I'll get a nurse to fetch you a fresh gown.'

Day 14 – Afternoon

●●●

Not for the first time, recently, I feel trapped. My gown might be fresh and clean, but it's hardly street wear, definitely not the height of fashion and tends to be a bit draughty around the back.

The little nurse, Mahalia, has been back and she seems really kind, but has obviously been told not to answer any questions about my health. She did tell me that since she's been at this hospital, she and her husband like to take country walks in the nearby lanes, all so different from her home in the Philippines. When I described where I had been in the woodland, she recognised it instantly. They walk that cinder path over to an old WWII airfield where they take their little boy to fly model planes his dad makes for him. It's the best place for that because there's a large area clear of trees and the family only live in a small flat, without a garden. They've seen foxes and roe deer there, too, in the reclaimed cultivated area, and once watched a pair of hares boxing. It shouldn't be hard for the police to find, in that case. Why isn't anything happening? Hasn't anyone told them?

I can hear Laura Coles voice down the corridor. Not long now. I will tell her I want to discharge myself and ask for my few clothes back. The door is opening.

'Hello Anna. Doctor Kensington tells me you've come on really well and should be strong enough to go home in a day or two.'

It seems they are slowly pushing back my release from hospital confines, one day at a time. Well, that's not happening.

'Before you start, Laura,' I say, 'I understand your concerns that the story I told you sounds farfetched, but it is all true. I was held captive, in an unbelievably cruel manner. I did have to overpower my captor to escape, and I did get lost in the woodland, before passing out at that field gate in the lane. Tuppence Halfpenny Lane, I was told by the police constable who came to see me.' The last few words are to show my memory's fine. 'I must write to Cecil, the lad who found me. Cranberry Farm is just up the hill, at the top of the lane, he said.'

'Well, we can sort that out as we go along, but for now I want to talk about some mild medication and arrange a regular appointment with a psychiatrist near your home.'

'Hold on, I can stop you there,' I flare at her. 'I am not taking any medication that doesn't come on a warm plate in a good restaurant. My only deficiency is the good nourishing food that was stolen from me by Patrycja. If anyone needs mental health care, it's her. All I need from you is to find a nurse who can bring me my clothes so that I can leave here before tea-time. I'm discharging myself if you won't do it.' My inner rage is winding itself up and I am struggling to keep calm and rational.

'Anna, let me be the best judge of that. That's what I'm here for. You must remember that you arrived here barely clothed, with no money, no phone, no means of proving your identity, claiming loss of memory, kidnap, and escape, and giving us only your name, before you had

had a night to recover and could tell us more. I'm sure you can see why we have to make absolutely sure you're fully recovered.'

Oh, that false, simpering, softness in her voice, when I can see in her eyes that she wants to slap me. To make me toe the line. To control me, just the same as Patrycja, though may be in a kinder way. My eyes dart to her hands, wary that she might have a syringe tucked in her palm, primed with a sedative. She hasn't. I relax a little and put myself in her place. I can see why she would be concerned. I'm not the usual vagrant hauled from some hedgerow ditch.

Taking a deep breath, I lean slightly forward, before holding Laura's eyes in a purposeful stare. 'I know you want the best for me, I know you find it difficult to believe my story, but the most import matter now is that I leave this hospital long before this so-called Pat arrives to collect me. And that is what I intend, permission granted or not.'

'But surely you want to see your sister.'

'I have no sister. Nor do I have any parents. They split up and abandoned me, an only child, when I was ten. And just because I am the product of care homes and foster parents doesn't make me mentally impaired. I'm a senior manager in an international insurance company, which I think shows a decent mental capacity and resolve to study and achieve high qualifications beyond the average nutter.' I realise, too late, I'm becoming too vehement when Laura responds.

'But she'd heard you left your job, without notice and under a cloud, from what I gather, and you worked in one of their call centres, according to your sister. Do you really find what you just said completely rational, Anna?'

Yes, I worked in the same building as the call centre, but six floors above it. The rest is obviously Patrycja fiction.

I steady myself. 'I don't want to argue with you, Laura. I'm sure Stuart will be able to confirm my status. You have contacted him, I hope, I gave Nurse Barratt the contact details.'

'Oh, yes. But it must have been your sister's number you gave her, in your early confusion. It was she who answered the phone. She's asked to come in and bring you a few things you might need.'

'Well don't tell this supposed sister anything.' I don't say it, but it's obvious Patrycja hasn't told Stuart anything or he'd be here. And how come she was answering his phone? I'm sure I gave Nurse Barratt the right number.

Day 15

●●●

I tried to escape, last night. Just like in the movies. It turned out to be more a comedy than an action-packed drama.

The first problem was clothes. I don't think I'd have got far sauntering down the high street in just a hospital gown. Apart from freezing to death. I asked Mahalia if she knew where my own clothes were.

'They've been kept safe for you; we have a special cupboard behind the ward reception desk for a patient's belongings that can't go beside the bed. Not valuables. They go in a safe. You'll get them back when you go home and have clean clothes to wear.' Mahalia goes a little warm faced. 'I afraid yours are thought a little unhygienic to keep in your locker.'

'You mean they are filthy dirty and stink to high heaven,' I say. She gave an involuntary giggle but said nothing.

Problem two was knowing where I was. Mahalia told me we were close to the town centre and the station. If I needed a taxi, she would give me a number to call, but she understood, from Nurse Barratt, that someone was going to collect me when I was discharged.

Which leads to problem number three. I have no money or card to pay any fare. I know Stuart would pick me up from somewhere, but first I need to phone him. But not on the hospital ward. I need to make a reverse charge call from an outside payphone.

So, there was the plan. 1. Steal back my clothes. 2. Run outside. 3. Look for a payphone. Easy. Except it wasn't.

Nurse Barratt, or maybe the doctor, had insisted that if I go to the loo I should be accompanied, in case I faint again, so at night, when there were less staff on duty, I was encouraged to use a bedpan, should I need. So, being very compliant, very late in the evening I asked for one. I'd had plenty to drink and held back until my bladder was bursting. As soon as the nurse came back to take it to the sluice, I jumped out of bed, peered from my doorway to see that she had gone into the sluice and jogged up to the empty ward reception desk. Luckily it was unattended, and I quickly tried all the cupboard doors. I found stationery and a few odd bits of ward equipment in the open ones, but most were locked. Foiled.

But I was on the move, and I could see my way into the main ward where there were curtains around one bed, from which came the voices of two nurses trying to calm an anxious patient and farther down an elderly-looking lady who was out of bed and wobbling towards the patients' bathroom. I caught up with her, offering to help, picking up the dressing gown she had left lying across the end of her bed and offered it to her. She shook it off her shoulders, shouting 'Stop it Doris, take me home,' when I placed it there, so I carried on with it over my arm.

Leaving the lady at the entrance to the bathroom, I peered back out to see all was still clear, then I made a dash to the double doors that I guessed would lead out int a corridor, found the green button that unlocked them and sped through. Looking both ways, as I donned the dressing gown, I spied the lift, and walked casually over to press the call button. I heard the rumble of the lift arriving and a clunk as it stopped at my floor, a pause and then doors slowly opening, to reveal a porter with a young man in a wheelchair.

The porter asked if I was OK and I said I was just going back to my ward, on the floor below. He told me I should have used a different lift, winked, and said he'd pretend he hadn't seen me. The man in the wheelchair looked up, smiled, and said 'My mate here's a good 'un,' then blushed slightly.

I pressed the button for the ground floor – I'd been on the third – and waited in trepidation for the doors to close, hoping the lift wouldn't pick up any more passengers on the way down.

Exiting onto another long corridor I looked for exit signs to follow. There were only a few people around, most looked like staff busying about their tasks, one couple were visibly weeping, and another were coming towards me in outdoor clothing, worry written all over their faces. They gave me a strange stare. And I realised I was really going to stand out in my present garb and no shoes if I stepped outside.

There was a cleaner coming out of a door with a bucket and mop. It went through my head that were I in a TV drama, I'd force her back in, clout her with the mop handle and change into her clothes. But this was reality. Though she still had her use. I spied a security guard making his way towards me, so I opened a conversation with the cleaner, first asking if there was a hospital shop (which there was, but it closed at eight-thirty, after visiting hours) and then how did she like working there and where was she from (Romania), and the security man passed by.

Ahead I could see glass doors leading to the car park. If I could just get through those. I quickened my pace. Whatever my appearance I had to get out. The doors opened automatically, and I strode through. I couldn't believe my luck. Right next to them was a Perspex hooded pay phone booth. I picked up the handset and dialled 100, giving the operator Stuart's number and asking for a reverse charge call. I waited. The call was accepted, and I was put through.

'Hello Anna. I wondered when you would call.' The voice was not Stuart's. I slammed the phone back on its cradle.

Then another voice. 'Hello, Anna. I think you're wanted back on Ward 34.' I turned and saw a burly man and an equally sturdy looking woman, both in security uniforms. Smiling – but with that look that says they stand no nonsense. Which is what they got as I shot off, ignoring the painful chips of gravel digging into my bare feet. I slid between two closely parked cars and on into the next double row, dressing gown billowing and flapping behind me. In the reflection from a windscreen, I saw the security man was nearly within grabbing distance and spun sharply to my left between the fronts and boots of cars that were almost touching. It slowed me down, but it slowed his bulk even more. I didn't know where I was heading, except out through the barriers that I could now see ahead – and that's where it all went wrong. As I crossed behind an ancient Montego, the dressing gown caught on the exhaust pipe, bringing me to a sudden stop, just as the security woman, who had run down the free space between the parking bays, appeared in front of me, arms stretched out trying to catch my fall.

I lay in a crumpled heap, needing to gather my breath, as the equally breathless woman crouched down beside me and simply said, 'Now, Anna, do you think you can walk back or shall one of us fetch you a chair?'

I was taken first to a cubicle in A&E where my cuts and grazes, all minor, were cleaned and dressed, then escorted back to the third floor.

When nurse Barratt came on duty this morning, any doubts about me being a mental case had probably gone. She told me that my "sister's" visit had been put back until tomorrow, I was being lightly sedated and I should concentrate on getting a good rest.

Mahalia is here now, checking my dressings, my temperature and, I expect, my temper. She adjusts my pillows, asks me if I want a tea or coffee to keep me going until the trolley man comes around. He's a volunteer, looks about ninety, cheery as a Cheshire cat, with a quip for every patient – especially the ladies, so Mahalia tells me.

'Next time you want to go for a moonlight stroll, Anna, tell me first. I'll fetch you some shoes. But you'll have to jump the barbed wire first, this place is more secure than Belmarsh.' Mahalia has sincere sympathy in her eyes. She treats me as if she believes my story. Perhaps I can get a message to Stuart through her.

'If I want to write to someone, is there a post box in the hospital, Mahalia?'

'Yes. In the entrance lobby.'

But of course, I've no paper or envelope, nor money to buy a stamp.' She reads my mind.

'Would you like me to ask if your sister can bring in some notepaper and a pen?

'No, it's alright, thank you. I don't want to trouble you or her unnecessarily.'

'Perhaps I can find something for you then, but no promise.'

'As long as you won't get into trouble with Nurse Barrett. She looks a bit strict.'

'Oh, no. She's just very dedicated. I get on OK with her, most of the time. She doesn't worry me.'

I dozed off for an hour or so. Mahalia has just looked in.

'You awake now? You OK.'

I nod my head and smile. 'Nearly back to normal.' I say.

She walks across to the bed, glancing back at the door.

'I'll just slip this in your locker.' She holds up two sheets of notepaper, a pen and an envelope with a first-class stamp.'

'But I can't pay you. I've no money here.'

She shrugs her shoulders. 'No worry. You just give me the letter tomorrow and I'll post it for you. But no telling Sister. Our secret.'

Day 16

•••

I waited until after the ward changeover to start my letter to Stuart. I pondered whether to send it to his home or business address. It would stand out against business mail, easily spotted by Patrycja now she was on the same floor, yet if she was answering his phone, did she have access to his house? Toss of a coin, except I remember she had her slave in IT who'd messed with my phone and laptop. Most likely he'd done something similar with Stuart's phone so that it had been put on call divert, so Patrycja could intercept the ones that she was interested in. His home was the best bet. I can't imagine him letting her move in, even though that's what she wants, I'm sure.

I'm now reading it through, while keeping one eye open for the arrival of Nurse Barratt. I've kept it simple, described the basics of the last couple of weeks in as few words as possible and asked him to come and fetch me. Quickly. I only hope it does the trick. And it's not intercepted here or by Patrycja. Perhaps Mahalia is just humouring me and will hand it straight to one of the doctors. No. I don't really think that. She seems genuine and keen to be helpful. I seal the envelope and put it in my locker. And wait.

Nurse Barrett comes in on her own.

'Your sister will be here in about an hour. I just wanted to check you are all tidy and ready for her. Did a nurse bring in a fresh gown?'

'Yes, thank you. I've had a wash, tidied my hair and feel much fresher.' I accepted her referring to my sister without objection, and saw a slight, satisfied smile cross her face. 'Julie, before my sister comes,' I continue, 'Would it be possible to have a word with Doctor Cole? I've had time, now, to consider what she was saying more sensibly.'

Her eyes light up in victory. 'Doctor Cole is a very busy woman, but I'll see what I can do. Doctor Kensington will be seeing you before you go, so you can always ask him any questions you have, if she's not available.'

I've been left alone for ten minutes when Laura Cole breezes through the door.

'Barratt says you want to see me,' she says, 'I can only give you a few minutes, but how can I help?'

'First, I want to apologise for being so short with you, before. I was still finding my presence in hospital somewhat surreal. I'm ready to listen now and I don't feel I've given enough attention to your or Doctor Kensington's advice. And I don't feel I'm ready to go home, yet. My own stupid actions have shaken me; particularly the fact that I was capable of them. You've provided a chink of light in my darkness.' I'd been working on that phrase all night.

'Well, Doctor Kensington will be the final arbiter on that, and how urgently they need your bed, but I can see why a longer stay might be beneficial, for both of us. I'll mute it with him.'

I'm thinking an extra day or two buys time for Stuart to get here, even though I'm sure I'll still get the visit from my sister. I'm quite looking forward to it and finding out what she has been saying about me. At least she won't be able to physically drag me from my bed and I could even end up with some wearable clothes.

For the last half-hour, I've been thinking of Stuart. Remembering how close we had become. We kept everything strictly professional in the office but away from it we allowed our passion for each other to run wild. We didn't hide our attraction to each other, neither did we flaunt it. We mixed with our colleagues and friends freely, we partied with them, we invited them to dinners in the large country house Stuart had inherited from his father. He, too, came from a broken home. His birth mother took him away from her cantankerous husband, senior by a good many years, then lost an acrimonious custody battle because of her alcoholism. Two stepmothers later, his father died, but left mere pittances to all three of his one-time spouses. His joy was his son. Nothing else mattered. And his son had attained everything hoped of him, in business, as a sportsman and in the management of the small Bembrige Estate – the house, a modest vineyard and stables.

We had become inseparable. I had moved in. He had proposed. I'd accepted. Was that what tipped Patrycja into her evil abduction. I realise now he was part of her game plan to reach the heady heights of the boardroom, with a ready ally on her side.

My private room door has been left open, at my request and I can hear familiar voices approaching. One is Sister Barratt the other is my disowned sister, Pat.

Patrycja, calling herself Pat, appears in an elegant, steel grey trouser suit and cornflower blue blouse and a stylish grey cap setting off her vibrant bob of red hair. Just the thing to cover up the damage I'd caused on my escape. I hope it still hurts.

'Hello, Sis, I've been so worried about you. Sister, here, has been so kind to fill me in with what's happened, while you've been here. It must have been terrifying waking up in a strange place like this. Not at all what you've become used to.' She knows how to rub it in – and to milk Sister Barratt's sympathy. Not for me, for herself.

I remain silent and glance toward Sister Barratt, who offers to leave us alone for half an hour and I nod my head in agreement.

'Well, well, well, we have put ourselves in a pickle,' Pat continues while still in Julie Barratt's hearing. But I'm here again to sort everything out and you'll soon be settled comfortably at home again.' She pauses to be certain that Sister is well out of earshot and continues. 'That's not saying which home you're going to, of course.' Coldness returns to her eyes.

'It wasn't very friendly of you, Anna, to leave without saying goodbye. You caused me such pain, departing like that, but I guessed where you might end up even before that call to Stuart, that I picked up for him. He's distressed too, to know that you could abandon him without a word, leave him to salvage the mess you made with that important client you were supposed to see. You never turned up to the appointment or even apologised. Such a terrible girl, who deserves to be shown up for what you really are. Well, what I say you are, is perhaps more relevant.'

I still stay silent.

'Technology is a wonderful thing. Especially if you know the right man. One you can mould to your wishes. Your surprise holiday in Thailand looks so exiting. All those amazing photos you put on Facebook. It's so easy to borrow them off the internet, and no one realises. You've even managed to send three selfies, with a little help from Photoshop and some images from a recent real holiday of yours. Nobody is expecting you back for another two weeks at least, especially now you've no job to come back to. Fancy quitting by email, without telling a soul you were going. HR were not at all amused. They'll be sending you a bill for breach of contract expenses. But how are you going to settle that? You can't lay your hands on any money in your present state.'

Patrycja is positively gloating, stern faced with the control she thinks she has. Another face appears at the door and her face flips quickly back into a smile. It's Mahalia.

'You OK, Anna. You want anything. Or your visitor?'

'No thanks, Mahalia, but please meet Patrycja.'

Mahalia barely masks her surprise at the name. 'Hello. Good to meet you. Anna is coming along fine, I'm sure she'll be glad when she can go home though. I will leave you to talk. That alright Anna?'

I nod and say 'Yes, please. Patrycja can't stay long.' Thank goodness she didn't mention the letter, which I'm sure she came around to collect.

'I'll stay as long as I wish,' says Patrycja, regaining her position of control. 'In a way, you've done me a favour, running away like you did. Perhaps worth that nasty bump on the head. That timely phone call meant for Stuart helped, too. That gullible Sister Barrett was reluctant to say much, but when I said I knew a little of your history, your past episodes of mental breakdowns, your tendency to live in a fantasy world, she seemed most interested. Especially when I told her that Smithson wasn't your real last name, you were just plain Ann Smith. It would have confused and delayed their search for any medical records.

'But then that was my original aim. To drive you mad. Then to let you free with an implausible story and no real memory of your past. To have you sectioned and carted away at least until Stuart and I were married. Which shouldn't take me too long. He's such an innocent, trusting bedfellow. Or soon will be. He's already blocked you on his phone and social media, unaware that my tech buddy has already put a divert on his phone, so I can monitor any calls from you. It would have been perfect to whisk you back, today, but for some stupid reason they want to give you another assessment. To see if you are fit to be let out into the real world. I've promised to take care of you as only a good sister can.

'You, Miss Smith, are being closely watched, so there's no point in any more nonsense and when I collect you tomorrow you will do exactly as I say. Or? Well, you know how strict I can be on discipline.'

I still hold my tongue, as much as I want to explode in an expletive filled fury, telling her there is no way she will control my life. No way she will trap Stuart in her web. But silence tells her nothing. Gives no game away.

'I'll be off then, since you seem to have little to say for yourself. I've left some smart clothes with Sister Barratt. She'll give you them in good time to be dressed and ready for when I arrive. Make sure you are.'

Patrycja exits stage right, as I think theatrically, after her little performance.

Mahalia enters and I give her the letter to Stuart. She asks if that was the real Patrycja. I tell her yes, warn her she's dangerous and ask her to play along with anything she says.

'You can trust me, Anna. I am good at reading people. I have a good nose for the truth.'

Day 17 – Morning

●●●

Before she went off duty, last night, Mahalia put her head around the door and whispered, 'Letter posted.' I nodded and thanked her with my eyes, then beckoned her in. I asked her if she remembered the young PC who had visited me. She did. 'The one who thought you were a cattle rustler,' she laughed.

I've had an idea. I'll know later if it works.

I'm to be discharged about midday if Doctors Kensington and Cole agree. Laura Cole is on her way over to see me now. I have about ten minutes to get dressed in the clothes Pat brought in: a comfortable, bright emerald-green top, black jeans, matching green shoes and quality tights and underwear. Most likely to impress Nurse Barrett, more than me. I doubt I'll be allowed to keep them. There's no coat or outdoor wear, I notice, so she's not risking me running off anywhere far, this frosty looking sunny morning.

The Cole woman seems quite brusque when she arrives.

'I hope you're serious about taking my advice this morning. Staying here another day wasn't necessary, according to Doctor Kensington. He was quite happy to discharge you yesterday and he needs every bed he can get.'

I can imagine that Dr K has given her a polite ticking off for not sorting this out before, so I say 'I'm sorry Laura. You're being so good to me, indulging me a little perhaps, and I will be going home today. It's just that I want a little more advice on my options to improve my mental state and how I can get help locally.'

'I did try to explain before, but I recognise you weren't in the right frame of mind then. I've brought a couple of pamphlets that might help, and I will send a referral letter to the Mental Health Team in your area, with a copy to you, so that you know what I have said. Someone from the team will contact you and take your case onwards from there. Your sister has given us her address, where she says you will be staying while you complete your recovery. I'll send the copy there. It seems there are some discrepancies in the information you originally gave us, but that will all be checked out by the end of the day.'

And I will be checked before the end of the day, I'm thinking. I thank her for her help and advice, then she wishes me well and leaves.

I'm worried. Time is moving slowly, but it's inching far too close to when Patrycja is due to arrive. And she'll probably be early to make sure I can't do a last-minute flit. The clothes she brought me are a surprisingly good and comfortable fit and have really perked up my overall disposition. If only my last hope could happen, but there are no signs that it will. I fidget between perching on the bed and sitting in the chair, unable to concentrate. I suddenly remember that poor old lady's dressing gown I ran off with and walk around to the ward reception desk and ask how I can recompense her. I'm told that there hadn't been any noticeable damage, it was well-worn already and it had been laundered and given back. I said

I'd go and apologise but was told I had better not. The woman had dementia and it would only add to her confusion. So, I returned to pacing my cell, as my private room had become.

I step out and look at the clock on the main ward. Twenty minutes and I could be on my way out of here. I look around. Two of the nurses are occupied with patients, a third chatting to the cleaner, close to the double doors. There's no way I can make an early exit on my own and I realise something that reminds me of Patrycja's words "you never think far enough ahead". She had. If I did do a runner, in this bright emerald top I'd be easily spotted and picked up again.

The minutes tick slowly closer to my doomsday. I settle back in my room waiting the inevitable arrival of Patrycja. I'd put all my last hopes in Mahalia. I know that the letter was really posted too late to be of use, though I secretly hoped to get a phone call to the ward, from Stuart. Now, my last-ditch attempt for salvation is not going to materialise. I need to steady my breathing and accept the consequences; I must hold back the tears and brave my way forward without showing my fears.

My heart finally sinks when Mahalia puts her head around the door and announces, 'Your visitor is here.'

Day 17 – Midday

●●●

I stare at the blue uniform in awe. Thank you, Mahalia. The constable pulls up the visitor's chair close to mine.

'Miss Smith … son. We received a message at the station to say you wanted to alter the statement you made to me the other day. That you weren't completely honest and do have some information about cattle rustling. You do know there are penalties for wasting police time, don't you?'

'Yes officer, I do apologise, but I was in a state of shock before, and frightened of the consequences of saying too much.' I'm not worried about being charged with wasting police time; I just want out.

'So, what is it you have to tell me? Was, that fainting attack a ploy to pervert the course of justice?'

I can read from his manner that this is a young copper keen to earn his sergeant's stripes or even transfer to CID. He's trying to read whether I'm going to be truthful, or not. Good. He wants to prove his detection abilities are higher than he's probably credited for, and this could be his chance. Solving a longstanding crime wave.

'Oh no, officer, that was real. I'd been out too long and not properly dressed for a day of observation, and I'd been up all night too.' Time to gain a little sympathy. 'These rustlers are hard task masters. I've been very naïve and stupid. Now I need to tell the true story.'

The constable straightens his back, and opens his policy book, pen at the ready.

'Right Miss, perhaps you can elucidate me of who these people are and any residences where we can apprehend them.' He's trying to impress me, poor lad.

'Yes, but I don't feel comfortable doing it here. 'There are local people in the hospital who might overhear and tip them off that it's me giving information.'

'So, there are locals involved, then.'

I let his assumption ride.

'The thing is, now I've plucked up the courage to talk, it might be best if I had a solicitor with me, down at the police station. I've been discharged from the ward. You can have a word with Sister Barratt, and she will confirm that. Trouble is I don't have any transport to come down. I don't suppose you can take me there and, because I'm away from home, arrange a solicitor?' I give him my best lost waif look, eyes beginning to water. I'm conscious of the ticking clock, Patrycja almost due. I pray he's arrived by patrol car and not on a bike. And then my mind goes into free-fall. What if Patrycja is already here, already waiting for me? What if she intervenes? My recently refreshed mental state pictures me trying to escape her clutches, speeding downhill on the crossbar of the constable's bicycle.

There's a pause as the clockwork of his brain considers the options.

'Not quite normal procedure, but considering the severity of the possible crime, I'd like you to follow me, please. You are not under arrest, but I will make a note of anything you say.'

Relief! We find Sister Barratt at the ward reception desk and the constable duly announces he is taking me in for questioning on a serious matter he can't disclose. No asking for permission. No room for a refusal. And an aggrieved looking Julie Barratt just turns to me and hands me a pharmacy bag of medications, saying all the instructions are on the labels, but to phone her if I need anything explaining.

The police car is parked just a short way from the hospital entrance and as the constable puts his hand on my head to guide me into the back seat, I breath relief that Patrycja, my so-called sister Pat, has not yet arrived.

Day 17 – Afternoon

●●●

The interview room is windowless and has a stale odour of countless previous occupants, who have sweated under police interrogation. Nevertheless, it is still far more pleasant than that dark, dank coal cellar. I've been given a plastic cup of lukewarm vending machine coffee, and that does remind me of my recent incarceration, while I wait for the duty brief to arrive.

She proves to be a slim and attractive woman in her forties, shoulder length natural blonde hair and dressed in a close fitting mid-blue trouser suit that enhances her well-proportioned curves. Something to distract an interviewer's mind from the main task, perhaps. I explain the whole situation over the last weeks and why I wanted to be interviewed at the police station. She warned me that I could be in serious trouble if it's viewed as a time-wasting ploy and that the outcome would be judged on whether the abduction element was believed. She wouldn't commit herself to whether she believed me or not, just stating she was here to defend me on the facts I gave her.

I sit back and wait for the constable to return, together with a detective he said would conduct the interview. And I wonder to myself what Patrycja would now be doing, after obviously running up to Julie Barratt and finding out what was happening and where I've been taken. I doubt she'd looked ahead this far.

The interview is brief. I explain why I had returned to my original statement and watch the crestfallen constable sink back in his chair, from his previously thrusting posture. I apologise profusely, but stressed that my capture had been real, the abductor is known, and I am concerned I haven't been taken seriously. I tell them I don't want to be forced into making an official complaint, I just wanted someone to investigate my claims. They promise me they will. The detective dismisses the constable and takes me to a phone so that I can contact my bank and arrange for a small sum of cash from my account to be available at a local branch, to tide me over until new debit and credit cards can be issued. I wisely cancelled the existing ones, after a lengthy security process which relied on my memory of several past statements. What joy that my memory processes have returned so completely.

I now have to find my way to the branch, apparently a twenty-minute exposed walk away. Twenty minutes of looking over my shoulder, a bright green beacon, before I have the money for a coach or a train fare. And a dark coat from the first fashion shop I find. Only then can I be sure to escape Patrycja's clutches.

I get to the bank without incident, and I'm marched to a glass side cubicle – where other customers can gaze in and wonder why, but not hear – for more security questions posed by a suspicious minded bank teller. Then I'm marched back to the counter, where he hands over the agreed sum, with barely a smile. He's another one who, maybe, thinks I'm nuts.

For the first time in weeks, I feel I'm in control of my life. Now off to buy that coat to cover up my bright green top. Maybe I can swap that too, for something more subdued. I'd spotted a fashion shop on the way to the bank, just two minutes down the same street. As if to complement my mood a shaft of sun breaks through the day's scudding clouds, a broad stripe of light on the bank floor, just as I walk to the doorway, and step aside to let in a young couple who, from a snatch of their conversation, are hoping for a loan to buy a bigger car. Glancing down at the girl's bump I can see why. All of which distracts me from the car that has drawn up outside. With two people in it I recognise. Patrycja and Laura.

Laura is already half out of the car before I can take it in and react. And Patrycja's choice of shoes for me, with very high heels, aren't going to help me run. Another forethought of hers. I step back inside. Surely, they won't want to cause a scene in here. But Laura swings through the glass door before it has time to close – and I'm trapped.

'Now, Anna, we don't want a scene in here, do we. Your sister told me you had run off to the police station, though what you expect them to do I can't imagine. You're not fully well yet, you need care still, which is why we thought a few days with your sister would allow you to relax in a homely atmosphere. Why don't you just come to the car, and we can get you settled in.'

I don't know how so-called sister Pat persuaded Laura to join her in her hunt for me, but I do know she has a very persuasive tongue and no doubt threatened action against the hospital for losing a vulnerable patient.

'It's quite a journey home for you, anyway,' Laura continues. 'It's best you have company. We phoned the police station and explained that you had had a collapse that put you under severe mental strain and they told us you were coming here to collect some money. I'm glad we arrived in time; you could have ended up in goodness knows what trouble, had you travelled off somewhere in the state you are in. The police were very understanding and promised not to take any more action against you or on what you told them. They were already suspicious when they checked your home address and found out that a person with the name you gave was on holiday in Thailand.'

'Alright, Laura, I'll come with you.' My tone is suitably dejected. I meekly follow her to the door. What else can I do? She goes through first, blocking any escape before she can guide me to the car. It's on double yellows, I notice, but not a traffic warden in sight. I despair. Then I remember my shoes and as I pass around Laura, who has opened the rear passenger door for me, while securely holding one of my arms just above the elbow, I jab a heel hard into her toes, kick off both shoes and run.

Day 18

●●●

I'm on a bus. I'm not sure where it's heading, as it drives through a countryside of meadowland and open views to a horizon of softly rising green hills. The driver was annoyed I didn't have the correct change and was not allowed to give me any, he said. I sit as close to the front as I can, prepared for a hasty exit, but so far there's proved no need. I should be able to relax, but my stomach is knotted with fear, as well as queasy from a hurried breakfast, and my legs feel like jelly still, after that sharp sprint from the bank, down a short alleyway and into a local market, that proved my saving. It was crowded enough to weave my way into the throng, away from any pursuer's gaze and once I was well surrounded, I tucked myself into a stall that sold hoodies. Teenager stuff screened with rock band logos. I chose one that I'd already seen three other people wearing, as I pushed my way through the milling townsfolk (perhaps the band had a local connection), thinking that that might add a little confusion, if my pursuers were still on the hunt and had found out what I bought. Unlikely, I know, but I'm up for anything that helps my getaway. It was a lot cheaper than buying a coat, and the next stall had cheap trainers in my size, which was a relief, though my feet are still sore from their pavement pounding.

In order to get a bed, last night, at a small B&B in a residential road, I lied that I was hiking, my rucksack and walking boots had been stolen and, more honestly, I was left with just the clothes I stood up in and a little cash. The lady proprietress took pity on me, found me the smallest room I've ever slept in (from choice) and took her payment in advance. This morning, she told me where to get a bus, during a breakfast of undercooked bacon and hard yoke fried egg, and suggested I hurry along to avoid missing it.

The local bus driver says his terminus is where the National Express coaches stop, so I can travel on from there, if not straight home, to somewhere I can change to the right route.

The bus has seen better years, and the gears grind in protest at being changed down for a steep hill, but it's no doubt a stalwart friend of the local community. Over the brow a small town comes into view, which will mark the end of this stage of my journey.

Alighting from the bus I can see a coach stand with a sign for National Express and I cross over to find a timetable. For once the gods are with me. Well almost. I'm on a direct route home. But not for another two hours. Two hours of shuffling around, one eye open for a cruising red Discovery Sport, so the first call for me is a chemist to buy a washcloth and some make-up. There's a public convenience by the coach stand, so I pop into the ladies and freshen myself up. Looking in the mirror, I at last seem to be a real person again.

It's close to lunchtime and I find a McDonalds. A cheeseburger and fries take away the lingering flavours of breakfast. I'm not fussy about my weight, today, after the enforced Patrycja diet and a few meagre portions of hospital food. With still time before the coach arrives, I buy a couple of supermarket ready meals, a small whole grain loaf and a bottle of milk, plus a strong plastic carrier bag. Padded out with a few non-perishables already in my old apartment, which I haven't got around to letting yet, such was the euphoria of moving in with Stuart, (and that for only a couple of weeks, before all this happened). It should tide me over for tonight and tomorrow. From there, I will go back to Stuart's, cleaned up and in my own clothes – albeit from the ones that I'd left behind to go to a charity shop.

Another look of surprise when I pay cash for my coach fare, but this time I can sit further back and relax. I'm on my way, and I can already feel my head starting to drop with tiredness.

Day 19

●●●

There's nowhere quite like your own bed. Especially after a traumatic ordeal that has lasted weeks. I was still dog tired when I arrived back and glad that I hadn't gone straight around to Stuart's. He'd have welcomed me and pampered me, I'm sure, but I was too exhausted to explain all that's happened and how I've arrived back. And the danger we are both in from Patrycja, for I'm sure she will seek vengeance on both of us. She may have muddied the waters with my supposed mental incapacity, but she'll know that that can be disproved, if she can't get to me first.

I was relieved to find my apartment seemingly as I left it, before moving in with Stuart. I had half expected to find her there, but then she would more likely expect me to run back to Stuart's arms for protection. And she would hope she'd discredited me enough for him to reject me. Maybe she has. It won't be long before I know.

In the meantime, as my landline is still connected (something else I must change), I've reported my phone and laptop as stolen and will order a replacement phone from a different service provider once my new bank cards come through. They'll be sent to this address. Once back with Stuart, I'll be able to access my social accounts and erase all Patrycja's fraudulent posts, pending recovering my laptop or getting a new one.

I'm not going to phone Stuart on either of his numbers, before I go over. I'm too scared who might answer. I've another puzzle on my mind. How come Patrycja was able to spare me all that time, albeit in short visits when it took me two and half hours to get back here form the vicinity of where I was incarcerated? And then it twigged. Those on the top floor are granted extended leave to work from home, provided they attend at least two internal meetings a month and maintain their presence at scheduled video conferences. And that explains her brief absence, while I was, in all senses, still in the dark. She had to report in, in person. It also means she could be roaming around now, work laptop by her side spying for another opportunity to grab me. That must not happen.

I'm tempted to phone the office to say I'm coming back in, in a couple of days, but if I'm to believe Patrycja, that might not be feasible. I'm supposed to have quit, according to her.

Having had a good long shower, a decent brunch, and copious cups of real coffee, I've sorted out a reasonable ensemble from the charity box clothes and I'm ready to face my reunion with Stuart. He'll be working all day and should finish by six. That gives me all afternoon to put my memories and thoughts in order and write out in longhand a complete story of events that I can take to the police. This time they must believe me. I know a couple of the officers from the local police station, so my identity won't be in question, nor my status and reputation.

It takes time, with several wholesale revisions and rephrasing of paragraphs to get it concise yet detailed. There's a gap I still can't recall which suggests which drug Patrycja used on me initially. Rohypnol. The generic one without the blue dye, or I might have spotted it. I vaguely remember her coming to see me and I remember waking in complete darkness, but all the time in between and how I was transported there is a complete blank.

Time to go. It's bright outside; the sun, now low in the sky, has been shining most of the day. A good omen, perhaps. I'm looking forward to surprising Stuart with my return, though with some trepidation as to how that will be received. How badly has his mind been poisoned by the scenario invented by Patrycja? Once I've paid my taxi fare there, I will have little money left from what I withdrew from the bank. But hopefully I can borrow one of his two cars (I don't know where mine is now), the VW Golf, not the Porsche, and tomorrow I can drive down to my own branch and withdraw a little more from my deposit account.

The taxi takes the scenic route, as always. I know a much quicker way, but I'm almost home. My new home with Stuart. There's a tree lined gravel drive running in a gentle curve up to the house and, as I approach the wide parking area separating the house from its four-car garage block, what I see makes me gulp. Two police cars, blue lights pulsing, a crime van, a policeman rolling out blue and white tape, another walking towards the drive, waving down the taxi – and a bright, metallic red, Discovery Sport.

There's no turning back.

Day 19 – Evening

●●●

I step out of the taxi, a blank expression on my face, not knowing whether to laugh at the irony of the scene before me, or cry, because my return looks as if it had been thwarted. Why are the police here? To arrest me? Surely not Patrycja. I can't raise my hopes that high. Or is Stuart in trouble?

Before the uniformed officer can speak, I brazen out that vain hope. 'Are you here to arrest Patrycja Sniegov, officer?'

'Hold on miss, before anything I need to know why you are here.' The officer gives a stern, but not unfriendly stare, with just a hint of a smile, his intelligent brown eyes weighing up who I might be. 'We can talk about why we are here later, if necessary, or if there's nothing to concern you, I'm afraid I must ask you to leave.'

'I'm just returning home from a stay in hospital, so I think all this will concern me.' I'm trying not to sound too officious, but my nerves are jangling, my chest tight with anxiety.

'Home? You're saying you live here? And your name is?'

'Anna Smithson. I'm Stuart Bembrige's fiancée. We live here together.'

'Hmm, Miss Smithson.' He's writing my name on the clipboard he's holding. 'I think you need to speak to the officer in charge. I suggest you pay your taxi fare and then follow me.'

I do as he suggests, and he guides me forward, walking alongside me silently, except for the steady crunch of boots on gravel, up to the front entrance to the house.

'If you can just wait here for a moment, miss, I'll fetch DI Henderson. He'll want to talk to you.'

Just inside the front door is a uniformed policewoman, who steps forward and gives me a sorry look. She's taller than me and looks very fit and probably slim beneath her armoury of equipment and stab vest. A sure deterrent to making a hasty exit. But that's not on my mind. I want to know what the hell is going on. Patrycja must be inside, she'd not in her car, and so must Stuart be. Has one of them had some sort of accident? There's no ambulance, but I can hear the steady aah-waah, aah-waah of one in the near distance. Is it coming here?

I move to go into the house, but the strong arm of the policewoman stretches in front of me.

'Not just yet, luv. Someone will be out in a moment,' she says. 'You look a bit shaky; would you prefer to sit in one of the cars.'

Yes, I'm thinking, in the red Discovery, so that I can see if there's anything in there to help me solve this ongoing riddle. But I just say, 'No thank you, I'm fine; just a little puzzled and taken aback to find the police here.'

Then any decision is taken away as a pudgy little man, in black wax jacket and fawn check trousers, literally skips down the front step and waves his warrant card within an inch of my face. Must think I'm short sighted, whereas, so far, it's the police I've already spoken to who suffer from that affliction.

'Detective Inspector Henderson. Sam Henderson. I'm told you are Miss Anna Smithson, and you say you live here, is that right?'

'It is. So, can you please tell me what's happened; why you are here. Is Stuart alright?'

My stomach flips as the expression on the DI's face changes from friendly bland to distinctly grave. I expect the worst before the words hit me. I can see he's watching closely how I react as he softens his voice and says, 'Sorry Ms Smithson, but Mr Bembrige died earlier today. Ms Sniegov found him when she returned home from work.'

I think the word home is even more painful than died. What has she done? Has she inveigled her way into Stuart's life or is this some twisted ruse?

The DI takes my silence as an opportunity to continue. 'I know that's upsetting news to hear and if you want to take a moment you can come into the hallway and sit down. I think our crime scene folk can cover a chair for you, and I need to ask you a few questions. I think you must know why.'

'Sorry, detective inspector, but I don't. Can I see my fiancée, first, please? And how did he die?'

'Aah, that won't be possible for a short while, I'm afraid. Our crime team has to finish its work first. There's another problem, too. I have to establish quite who you are.'

I go to speak but he holds up his hand. 'Bear with me, but what you told the constable, before, doesn't quite square with what Ms Sniegov has told us. She claims that she is his fiancée and shares the house with him, though the latter has only been in the last few days. So, you turning up unannounced presents me with a quandary. Who should I believe?'

'Well not that evil, scheming, lying bitch, that's for sure.' I immediately realise that flaring up like that won't help my case. I ball my fists tightly and breath deeply to try and bring myself under control, while half of me wants to push past this rotund little man, find Patrycja and wring her scrawny neck.

'Miss Smithson let's try and be calm about this. You can, I'm sure, see my dilemma. Two people claiming the same relationship. Two people saying they live here. Perhaps you have some form of identity on you to help prove who you are.'

But of course, I haven't. I explain that my bank cards, driving licence and everything else of mine was stolen, saying it was while I was in hospital. Then I explain the reason I was in hospital but only telling the story from the time I fainted in Tuppence Halfpenny Lane, skirting around my memory loss, other than from my collapse. He seemed sympathetic, but also unconvinced. Then I remembered that my car should be in the garage, a blue Mini Cooper S Convertible, hoping Patrycja had returned it there after abducting me. Hidden in plain sight, so to speak. It would be like her to do that. I realise, too late, after I'd told him the registration, that it is still registered to my old address. I tell him that, too, as one of the constables trundles off to open each of the garage doors. He comes back and quietly says something to the DI.

'If you're telling the truth, Miss Smithson, it seems your car has been stolen, too.'

Day 20 – Morning

●●●

I thought I'd be more settled to confinement by now but sitting on this hard bench in a holding cell is definitely unsettling. The words keep circling my brain, as trapped in there as I have been in here, throughout the dark hours of the night.

'Miss Anna Smithson, I am arresting you on the suspicion of the murder of Mr Stuart Bembrige.'

When DI Henderson said those words, late last evening, I shuddered with fear, an ice-cold shiver tracing the length of my spine, my head reeling in disbelief, and beyond the detective's blue eyes that delivered this cruel joke, I recalled the icy stare of another pair.

I wasn't allowed past the hallway of the house and although I know Patrycja must have been in there, I did not hear or see her. The house is large (much too big for just one, Stuart always said). He had a cleaner and a gardener, though at weekends he loved to spend an hour or two working a vegetable plot to one side of the kitchen. It was a sunny spot and I enjoyed helping him – and hindering him, even more so. A tear rolls down my cheek as I realise I shall never do so again.

Last night's formal interview was brief. DI Henderson and a colleague whose name I didn't catch, asked questions about where I had been during the day, who could corroborate my movements and why I chose to be at my own apartment rather than the house I said I lived in. When I mentioned I'd had a long shower I noticed the other detective's eyes tracing my body and can imagine where his thoughts were at that moment.

I can see their problem. I carry no solid proof of identity, I give a spurious story of where I have been in the last few days and there's the plausible motive of being the jealous, discarded woman. I refused a duty solicitor, last night, but I've made my allowed call to bring in a legal representative from the firm that carried out the conveyancing on my apartment. I haven't met her before, but I've seen her name in the papers a few times regarding successful defences.

A uniformed policewoman fetches me from the cell and takes me to the same interview room as before. She explains how long I have with my solicitor, who is already seated, before DI Henderson conducts his second interview.

'Hello Anna, I'm Margaret Sears. Let's not waste time, make yourself comfortable – if that's possible on these wretched chairs. I'm sure they're rejects from some factory canteen. Tell me everything you can, you haven't been charged, but it is a serious crime being investigated and every little detail will help.'

I barely have time to recount the past few weeks when the door opens and the smiling tub of DI Henderson enters, with his colleague, and announces 'Times up ladies. We've a crime to solve.'

The two detectives settle themselves opposite. 'Good morning to you both. I see you've engaged the formidable Ms Sears, Anna. You must be worried.'

'Wouldn't you be when you are accused of a murder you didn't commit'. I get a nudge and a stern look from

Margaret Sears, who has told me to just answer questions, and no more, and to use my right to make no comment, if the questioning gets too aggressive.

But the contrary is true. After announcing names and time for the recording (I now know the other man is DC John Wright) DI Henderson asks me to refresh his memory of my recent whereabouts. Which I do (skipping over the long shower) and tell them I have a much fuller account, in writing, at my apartment, which includes details about my abduction by Patrycja Sniegov, my stay in hospital, and my reporting the full story to the police local to the hospital, which they seem to have discounted without further investigation.

The DI leans right forward. 'Miss Smithson. Why didn't you tell me about this last night? May I suggest a night in a cold cell has given you ample time to dream up a story that you hope we'll take in and that is purely meant to divert attention from yourself to a former colleague, for whom you bear a grudge for running off with your man.'

I glance at Margaret. 'No comment.'

'Oh, so we are going to play the silent game, are we?'

Margaret intervenes. 'Miss Smithson will be happy to answer any legitimate questions, detective inspector, based on evidence you have acquired, but not on spurious suppositions intended to intimidate. Would you like to continue, please?'

'Madam, I am doing the interviewing and I shall use whatever means I feel necessary to establish the truth.' The DI is asserting his role as investigator.

'In that case, detective inspector, may I politely suggest you outline what evidential basis you have to be even questioning my client.'

'That is something I am about to do, having established Miss Smithson's account of where she was during the time that Mr Bembrige met his death, under suspicious circumstances.'

I haven't been told yet how Stuart died, and I'm tempted to ask, but Margaret has advised me to say nothing unless in answer to a question. Let them do the digging, she said, we might find a hole big enough for them to fall in.

'Miss Smithson,' the DI continues, 'you appear to be an intelligent woman and you seem, so far, to be cooperative, but I have to establish the veracities of your responses. For instance, you willingly gave us the name of the hospital in which you stayed, but you failed to mention that your brief residence there was because of a mental health episode that affected your memory. We do check these things, you know. So, am I right that you suffer from memory losses?'

'No, you are not right, detective inspector,' I reply, keeping my calm despite inner turmoil, 'I suffered a temporary memory loss through, I believe, being drugged and then held captive in an unlit coal cellar for several days and my memory has returned without impairment except for that drug induced period in which I was abducted.'

'And you didn't think this was important enough to tell me yesterday? May I put it to you, with Ms Sears' permission, of course, that what you think are unimpaired memories might not be as accurate as you hope. That whatever trauma you must have suffered to land up in hospital has indeed affected your recall. Furthermore, you failed to mention that you agreed, according to the hospital, to go and stay with the woman you believed was Ms Sniegov, for a period of rehabilitation. Hardly what one would expect if she had kept you against your will. Is that so Miss Smithson?'

'That agreement was forced on me, detective inspector and as you will know I never let it happen.'

'Yet you turn up at the home of Mr Bembrige and Ms Sniegov, where surly she would have brought you. That seems contradictory to your running away. But let's not dwell on that. Let's look at your uncorroborated statement of your whereabouts leading up to your arrival at that house and compare them with the evidence – yes, evidence, Ms Sears – that we have in our possession.'

I stay silent. I need to hear what evidence they think they have.

'You told us yourself, Miss Smithson, that you owned a blue Mini Cooper S convertible, and you will be pleased to hear we have traced that for you. It was parked just around the corner from your own apartment. And what is more, we know that it was driven from Mr Bembrige's house yesterday afternoon at 12:27 pm. Did you forget, Miss Smithson, that there is CCTV security around the house that records twenty-four hours a day? And yesterday was bright and sunny, yet you leave your soft top up, I notice, and the pictures are clear enough to see you've still got the hood up on your hoodie. After your tale, I'd have thought you would want as much fresh air and freedom as you can get. Unless you didn't want to be seen. And the fact that one of the tapes appears to be missing, which might have recorded your arrival, also suggests that.'

I push back into my hard chair, astounded. Not just because it wasn't me driving, it's the audacity of somebody just driving away in my car. Somebody who had my car keys. Someone easy to guess. Someone who could have taken whatever of my possessions she wanted, while I was unconscious. Someone who wanted my car to be seen leaving, but not what time it arrived, in case I was still travelling back then.

Margaret is quick. 'So, you are saying you saw someone driving away in my client's blue car with a hoodie obscuring her head. Might I suggest, this time, you could be premature in assuming it was my client if the driver's face was not in full view?'

Apart from a hard stare, The DI's response was non-committal. 'It just seems strange it was parked so close to your client's home, don't you think? But that's not the most damning of evidence that has come to our notice. Miss Smithson, do you have any habits we should know about? Recreational habits, particularly of the powdered kind?'

I know what he's asking. and the answer is simple. 'I regularly run and the only powder I take is in a protein drink.'

'You don't have a drug habit or access to them, per chance, then.'

'No. I've always abhorred them. I saw what they did to some of my student friends when I was at college.'

'That's strange, considering what was found in your car. But we'll come back to that later. I can say no more to you, for the time being. Not until blood analysis and toxicology reports are complete.'

Now, that's something he wants to leave hanging over my head, to break me down. I won't let that happen. Whoever moved my car could have planted anything that might incriminate me, knowing it would be difficult for me to disprove.

Suddenly, he terminates the interview and when asked by Margaret what was the cause of death, he hides behind waiting for the result of the post-mortem.

Day 21 – Evening

●●●

I can't understand why this morning's interview ended so abruptly. That man obviously doesn't believe me. Then, of course, Patrycja got to him first and must have thrown all sorts of doubt over my character and mental stability. I need to find something more positive to prove what's happened. To prove I'm the sane one. But for the moment that vindictive woman holds all the cards. No doubt with support from Doctor Laura Cole when that's needed.

This cell is more claustrophobic than the coal cellar, even though it's light. I can't see out of the high narrow window of square glass bricks, the walls are bare and there's nothing but my thoughts to keep me company.

How did I get into this mess? I should be free and Patrycja facing a long jail term. There must be something else to tip the balance that I need to bring to the front of my mind. One thing, that's all I need, to prove my relationship with Stuart. Oh, poor Stuart, what has she done to him? My heart sinks to think of him, no longer alive. The tragedy of him lain out somewhere in the house, with no one to help him. If only I'd gone over sooner in the day, things might have been different. But finding Patrycja there before me; it should have been me discovering him, holding him, helping him, being there at his last even, rather than hearing that blunt divulgence by DI Henderson. The dumpy man has no heart. I only hope he has a brain. That he can follow the clues, realise it's Patrycja that needs to be behind bars and end my misery.

I'll miss Stuart, he had a full heart, he was so trusting, so kind. Patrycja will have taken advantage of that. But how could he let her move in, even if she fed him lies about me. The police are being too slow, jumping to the easy conclusion, prodded in that direction by a vindictive mind.

When will they say how he died? The DI mentioned toxicology. Was he poisoned? Who would do that? He was so well regarded at work, in his local community, and his sports club. How could he have enemies? Who could he have upset to such a degree they wanted to murder him? And why do the police think it's murder? What did they find?

I'm summoned back to the interview room. What's it going to be this time? I'm told Margaret Sears will be there, so it's going to be important. Am I going to be charged?

Same blank walled room, same hard chairs and same two faces staring at me, one announcing the date, time, and our presence for the recording.

'Good evening, Miss Smithson, I'm sure you're as tired as I am of going over the same old ground, but it's all part of out procedure to grind out the very essence of truth from the different statements of you and others. So, forgive me if some of my questions sound very familiar.'

They are. And so are my answers, except I say them with less anxiety, now I've accepted there is little more I can offer. DI Henderson seems a little more satisfied with them, this time, perhaps because they have not changed in any noticeable content.

'Are you sure that there is nothing more you can tell me, Miss Smithson? Any little detail that could add to our enquiries, no matter how small or insignificant to you, could make all the difference to us.'

'I can't think of anything. I just know I'm innocent. I know you expect me to say that. I just wish you'd believe me.'

Margaret leans forward looking the DI directly in the face. 'You and I know the time limits for keeping my client here for questioning. Are you going to formally charge Miss Smithson or, I as hope, have you the sense to let her go home?'

'And there's the rub, Ms Sears. Which home will she want to go to? The Bembrige residence is still a crime scene and so is Miss Smithson's. I'm sure another night in this four-star hotel should be adequate for her.'

'Less of your sarcasm, please, detective inspector. This matter is too serious to joke about and since you have not presented any firm evidence to associate my client with the sad death of Mr Bembrige, I suggest you release my client forthwith and, with her consent, I will arrange suitable accommodation for her and advise you of the address. May we have a few moments in private, please?'

'If you'll just let me ask a couple more simple questions, then we'll have finished for the time being. Then you can have plenty of time with your client. She's not going anywhere soon. So, Miss Smithson, would you say your relationship with Ms Sniegov was a good one, or was there a tension between you. You seem very keen to incriminate her, almost suggesting she would be capable of murder.'

'I always admired Patrycja, at work, for her forthright approach and ambition, so the only tension there was a competitive one between our two teams. And that was a good thing because it spurred them on to greater productivity. There never was any animosity between us.'

'Then put it another way, were you envious of her more successful rise to management and recent promotion to a position you thought you deserved?'

I glanced at Margaret, wondering if I should answer that. She mouthed, 'Be honest,' and after a brief dwell to gather my words I replied.

'I don't know who could have put that thought in your mind, detective inspector. I was disappointed, of course, but she deserved it for her hard work and perseverance; her leadership; her accomplishments for the firm. I was only too ready to congratulate her. I remember joking with her about having to have a new security tag for the posh doors upstairs.'

That's it, that's what I've missed. The proof that I lived with Stuart.

'Detective inspector. You've just triggered something. Stuart was very security conscious, as you've observed. Wisely so in his senior position. He had a small wall safe inside a cupboard under the kitchen sink. He insisted that we put our tags in there overnight in case we were burgled. I can give you the combination. You'll find my tag inside.'

I gave him the code, presuming he or another officer would go and look and, also, ask Patrycja if she knew about it – and the code. I'm sure she wouldn't. I don't believe she'd moved in. Stuart saw her in a different light than I did. That I know.

DI Henderson makes a note of what I'd just told him and switches off the recording.'

'I'll see you both again in the morning. Sweet dreams Miss Smithson.' With a sly smile the dumpy DI Henderson and the rather good-looking DC Wright leave the room.

Margaret Sears turns to me. 'I smell new evidence, Anna. He has changed his attitude. He is calmer and more receptive. I think he's made his mind up, but I can't be sure which way. But if he doesn't charge you in the morning, he'll have to let you walk out of here. And that's what we must both hope for.'

Day 22

●●●

I did manage to snatch some troubled sleep last night, having got used to the noisy arrivals of others brought into custody night and day (many drunk and most protesting vociferously), but the brightness of dawn awakened me early. There's nothing more I can do except await my fate. I pace the cell, and sit in silence, alternately, then do a few stretch exercises, before a breakfast of pasta bake, cereal bar and coffee is brought to my cell. Waiter service from a young constable in Henderson's four-star hotel! What more could I want. Maybe freedom?

At nine o'clock I'm shown into an interview room. A different one, though you'd hardly notice except the chairs are grubby blue vinyl covered instead of grubby brown.

DI Henderson walks in on his own, holding an iPad. 'You might like to see this.' He places it onto the table. I read the headline of local paper's Internet edition.

INSURANCE BOSS MURDER
NEW SUSPECT ARRESTED.
Unnamed woman dragged protesting
into police car as she swipes at officer.

There's a picture of an elegant woman, arms flailing and a policeman's cap in mid-air. I recognise the woman.

I sit back, not knowing how to react, what to say.

'You see, Miss Smithson, we are not quite as slow as you might think. We did check what you told us. All of it. And had some conflicting responses from people we spoke to. We also found the whereabouts of where you say you were incarcerated, a pool of excrement in the coal cellar, a short pipe in the doorway and signs of a scuffle. The hatch to the cellar was as you described it and the farmhand who found you confirmed that you were spark out beside the gate to a field of cows.

The hospital report threw a wobbly, the psychiatrist there convinced you had a mental problem and the police station you attended admitted they had not taken you seriously enough, because you had misled the young officer.

The bank confirmed you withdrew a sum of money, and the local bus driver remembers how pale and scared you seemed, sitting right at the front of the bus. The market stall holder also remembers you, particularly because you wore no shoes.

'Oh! And we spoke to your foster sister, Patricia, who said you were in a very confused state, still, when she saw you in hospital. She thought you believed she was your captor and not there to help. I can understand that, with the similarity of names.

'I can't comment on our new suspect, though I realise you will have recognised her from that photo. But the up-come of it all is that you will be released without charge, although I might want to question you again as a material witness. So, I should be grateful if you can keep yourself available for the next few days.

'You are unlikely to need Ms Sears again. Happy you've done your work here, Margaret?'

'Yes Sam, but I think Anna would like to know the cause of death.'

'Seeing as it's leaked into the public domain, we believe at this stage it was a drug overdose.'

I gasp. 'But Stuart has never taken drugs of any kind, for all the time I've known him closely.'

'That's what our enquiries suggest, which is why we are still treating this case as murder.'

I thanked Margaret Sears, went through the official procedure at the charge desk and walked out into the sunlight. I'd been told I could now go back to my apartment.

Eighteen Months Later

●●●

I enjoyed my time in court. As a witness. Try as the defendant's counsel might, he could not disprove the evidence I gave. I drew sympathy from the jury; I could see it in their eyes. And I watched Patrycja collapse as the foreman gave the verdict. Guilty. They all believed me. Then you did, didn't you?

It didn't all go quite to plan. Stuart wasn't supposed to die. I intended to arrive in time to save him. For him to be indebted to me forever for rescuing him from Patrycja's warped intention to step into his job by disposing of him. I must have miscalculated the dose, poor man, and Patrycja turning up before me was definitely not scheduled. I shall always miss him, though it's strange how life turns out. I'm married to a policeman now, just promoted to Detective Inspector. I'm Mrs John Wright. He's very protective. I feel so safe, now. And I've been promoted to a coveted top floor office, in charge of the lucrative legal firm insurance policies and fittingly remunerated. Patrycja's old job.

I knew Patrycja from my college days. We went out with the same group of undergrads, had good fun. She was a little shy at first, her Polish upbringing being quite strict, but a couple of months in she partied like she'd never known another life. She was popular, sought after by all the bed-notchers, flirtatious and fun seeking, yet holding a hard line against anyone who tried to get too close. Most of all, she was respected. Not like me. I was considered anyone's game, not without reason, until I followed her lead. She was a born leader, academically as well. I was a little envious then, but it made me strive harder to achieve and when we both chose a similar career and joined the same firm the competition became obsessive. For me anyway.

Initially, I faired the better, moving up the ranks faster, but after three years we were level. Four years and we both were team leaders in parallel disciplines, mine commercial insurance, hers primarily domestic. And her team, ruled with Dickensian strictness, was more productive than mine. We both had eyes on the floor above and we both knew the key was to impress Stuart Bembrige. Every way we could. And in no way was I going to let her win that prize.

Thinking (quite wrongly) her name might be holding her back, she mooted changing it to Pat White. Sniegov "means from the snow". I persuaded her not to, just nicknamed her Icy from thereon. It suited her cold and calculating demeanour. I intended to exude warmth towards Stuart.

Knowing Stuart ran frequently at a place quite close to my home, I took up running. I had to get noticed more than just as a bright office colleague. That tumble I mentioned did really happen, and the ride back in his luxurious car. But nothing serious developed from it. Not in the way Patrycja started to get her steely claws into him. By stealth. Unlike I would have done, she kept her emotional ties on a persistent low burn until she was offered promotion to the upper deck, alongside him – and two weeks later he proposed. That's when she told me that, despite her strict moral upbringing she was moving into his house at the end of the month. Apparently, up until then, she had never gone to his house at night (strange girl), so as not to sully his reputation (and, no doubt, hers, if it got back to her authoritarian parents).

Time for action. I could sense I'd reached my ceiling for years to come, if Patrycja won. I could look for another job, but there was nothing comparable elsewhere. I knew exactly where I wanted to be, and that wretch seemed to have got there first. She had to be discredited, locked away for life, before any nuptials took place. Preferably, before she even moved in.

The plan was straightforward, but quite testing to carry out. I knew of the old airfield, and its change of use, from an ancient aunt I used to visit in my pre-teen years, who lived out that way. She'd passed away since – natural causes, I assure you – and no one in the area would be likely to remember me or even notice me. I went up there and found the empty boiler room and coal cellar, in a building that was awaiting demolition. Perfect.

I was still friends with Patrycja and stayed over at her place a few times when we had had a late night out. It was on one of those that I stole an old hoodie she had hanging up and that she only wore to clear the snow in winter, so she had once told me. I can't remember why. It was tucked half behind other outdoor coats and jackets, so it was unlikely that she'd notice it was missing.

Now to the nasty bit. The bucket of excrement. I had to produce that myself and take it up to the coal cellar, in a hired car. I wasn't risking spilling it in mine. Or someone spotting my blue Mini. Making a mug of foul gruel was almost as bad, but the wooden lid to fit the bucket proved a more interesting task. I didn't know I had carpentry skills. I'd taken a couple of weeks off work, without notice, and during that time, rather than languish in a dark cell, I put my feet up at home and fed my social media with glorious pictures of Thailand. Even sent that email saying I quit. Patrycja never had a pet IT man, which is why poor DI Henderson could never get one to admit anything. He just thought whoever it was feared for his job and wanted it to stay secret. Wouldn't you?

All quite straight forward for setting up the venue for my supposed incarceration, now for the ingenious bits.

I was at home. I was comfortable, but I went on a strict diet of palatable, but nutrition deficient meals and beverages. I lost pounds. (I wonder if I could make money from that diet?) I did spend a night in the woodland. In a cosy sleeping bag, which is still stuffed irretrievably down a hollow trunk of a fallen tree. I'd already sussed out when the cows went for milking, and I collapsed (that lad thought) at the gate having wondered around in little more than nothing to get thoroughly chilled. I didn't like that bit much. The hospital stay was real, with a little play acting on my part. Wished I'd pinched the old lady's slippers as well as her dressing gown, that carpark was lethal on my feet.

The Pat who visited me wasn't Patrycja, of course, although she luckily had similar colouring, and it was her phone number I had given Nurse Barratt, though I'd said it was Stuart's. She was a sort of sister to me, at one of the foster homes in my teenage years and we had kept contact ever since. I'm afraid I played on her gullibility, pretending my mind was still a little wobbly, so she went along with anything I said, as she had once before. I was sixteen when I was knocked over by a speeding car. I did have a short loss of memory then, enjoyed the fuss and got her to keep secret that I was OK again, for a couple of extra months. That way I could get away with bits of mischief that wouldn't normally be tolerated. That help me play act this time. Anyway, in all innocence, she told the police she genuinely thought both my story was true, and I was suffering from name confusion from the trauma, when she came to the hospital. I'm so lucky I wasn't fostered with a Sue or a Jane or any other name.

The morning before my discovery by the farmhand, I'd been up to the coal cellar, spilled the foul-smelling bucket over the floor, left a mug of gruel there, dropped a length of pipe by the doorway and scuffed around with my feet, throwing one or two half bricks around for good measure. Pulled a few of my hairs out, too, and tossed those down. Painful, but it had to look authentic. I drove back home then returned by coach and local bus, sitting right at the back in both, dressed in a duffle coat with the hood up. That's stuffed below the sleeping bag, but it helped keep me warm for the night in the woodland.

My trip home, once I was discharged from the hospital, via the police station, was more leisurely than the police believe. That policeman's quest for cattle rustlers was a godsend, saved me being too inventive in my plea for help. I've still got that rock band hoodie and I can tell you of a B&B to avoid at all costs.

Oh, another little gem, to explain my absence from home, I'd told the guy in the apartment below me, that I was on standby for a night flight budget holiday in Thailand and if I suddenly disappeared, that's where I'd be. And that's what he told the nice WPC who called looking for me.

Of course, being at home most of the time, I could log in to the firm's electronic diaries. I knew Patrycja's login, and used that, so no checks would show it was me. Consequently, I knew when Stuart would be working from home and where Patrycja was supposed to be each day. Now this is where the greatest ingenuity was needed.

I looked up an old college contact of mine. Not a student. He used to supply me with a few recreational aids, shall we say. He didn't know my name, I always used a false one, Amy, and he could get anything for a fistful of cash. Including undied Rohypnol. Now all good plans benefit from a little bit of luck and mine had been a couple of weeks before Patrycja's promotion.

I was working late on an important presentation and phoned Stuart with a couple of queries. He invited me over to go through it and add the final polish. It was then he asked me to drop my office security tag in his safe. He was paranoid about late night intruders, he said, and he showed me where it was. I watched him open it, closely, and contrary to some of my story, I have a photographic memory, especially for numbers. Late in the evening, he offered me a glass of wine, I said just one, as I was driving, but once it was opened consumed most of the bottle. He was drinking whisky. It was late and, realising I would be over the limit for driving, he suggested that I stay over in one of his home's many rooms. I could drive back to my flat in the morning, change and go straight to the presentation from there. I hesitated, very briefly, and said yes. And that is what happened. To be honest I had hoped for more, but there was nothing forthcoming. When I left, after a light breakfast, I watched him retrieve the tag from the safe, reinforcing my memory of the code. I also had a quick word with his cleaner, as she arrived, a quizzical look on her face.

So, you will see, though it wasn't planned then, I had everything I needed for the final scenario.

Day 19 – Revisited

•••

There's nowhere quite like your own bed, after a few days away. But there's no time to luxuriate under a cosy duvet. I have much to do. I just have a breakfast biscuit and one cup of freshly ground coffee. It's easier to act hungry if you are hungry. Then I check the firm's e-diary to make sure Stuart's and Patrycja's plans for the day haven't changed. Stuart is working at home, with a conference call early morning, and another late afternoon. I've a four-hour window in between. Patrycja is going to a client meeting miles away. I doubt if she'll be back before dark.

I put my flat in order, leave my extended written statement on the kitchen breakfast bar, pen at the side, as if I have just finished it, then make my way down to the car, wearing an old dress with large patch pockets and a dark hoodie. It's parked a couple of streets away, out of view from nosy neighbours. It's quite a short drive over to Stuart's place and I pick my time to arrive after his morning business call.

Driving up the long drive I think this could still be mine, but that is secondary to my intentions. Lady luck is sitting on my shoulder, today, and I see one of the garage doors is open. I drive straight in, so the rear of the car faces the house, then walk up to the front door and pull back the ancient brass doorbell in its ornate circular escutcheon. Stuart is in for a surprise. He's dispensed with his cleaner (he found her pilfering) and has an industrial company send odd bods around every couple of weeks, so he comes to the door himself and swings it back.

Oh, the look on his face. A contortion of amazement, loathing, anger, and concern flashing across it.

'Where the hell have you been? What on earth's happened to you? You look a wreck. Sorry. I shouldn't have said that. You better come in. And explain yourself.' His words tumble out as the shock of my sudden arrival hits him. He's angry.

'You shoot off to Thailand on a whim, you quit your job without notice, leave a pile of jumble in my house and you turn up at my door like some waif or stray. What for? Hoping for forgiveness? Well, that's going to be hard won, if you get it at all. Coffee? You look as if you need one.'

Armadillo man. Underneath that hard shell is a softness that always wins through. 'Come into the kitchen. I was about to take a break, so let's see what's really been going on.'

I must regain his trust, so I put on my best sorry face and explain I have been in hospital after a sudden collapse, and someone has hacked my social media and my emails. I've never been to Thailand, ever. My hospital stay involved transient global amnesia, but I have recovered my memory, now. I tell him I'm at a loss as to why all this has happened and want to put matters right.

'To start, I can remove my jumble, as you call it,' I say. He smiles. One that lights up his eyes.

'I was certainly thrown by what appeared to happen. So out of character. I asked Patrycja if she knew anything, if you had any problems, but she said you seemed perfectly OK the day before you disappeared. Mind you, I find your explanation hard to take in, but I'm only too relieved that you are safe and well. And of course, I'll get HR to sort out what happens about your job, assuming and hoping you want to come back.'

'I do.' I take a sip of the coffee he's made me as we talked, which is now going cold. 'Aren't you having a coffee, Stuart?'

'No, I like to have a rehydration drink at this time of day. Keeps me alert better than a caffeine hit.' He walks over to a cupboard and takes out a glass, fills it with cold water and drops in an effervescent tablet. Perfect.

'Right, he continues, do you need another coffee? That must be cold by now.'

'Stuart. I don't want to impose on you. I shouldn't really have come. But I wanted to explain to you first. You're more understanding than most. I thought I'd have a better chance of telling the truth without too many interruptions and dubious looks. And I feel better now that I've done that. Perhaps I should take my jumble and go.'

'No, don't rush off. Let's see if we can come up with a plan to ease you back into work. I'll square it with HR and I'm sure your team will provide full support. They miss you; look up to you – even if one or another of them is hoping to get your job! Have a hot coffee. I think I can find some biscuits, too.'

Even more perfect. While Stuart rummages in his cupboards I dose his drink. As we talk over the coffee and biscuits, I watch him become drowsy. Quite soon, he says he's feeling queasy, all of a sudden, can't understand why and goes and sits on a sofa in the living room, later asking me to draw the curtains across as the light is hurting his eyes. He passes out soon after that. He's a strong man, it took longer than I hoped. But he's in the right place. Then, I did guide him there. There's a glass topped coffee table in front of him and I fetch out the supplies from my deep pockets and cut a couple of lines of cocaine on it, mess it up as if there'd been more, drop a straw on the floor and with another straw, blow a quantity up his nose. I give him a quick kiss on the lips and whisper 'Sweet dreams.'

I must work fast, now, and the first task is to find where the CCTV is recorded. I know it's an old system, Stuart commented it was time he changed it when I came around that time, some weeks ago. I find it in a cupboard on the landing and it's the type that takes tapes. Alongside are several numbered cassettes which he obviously uses in rotation. I erase the current one and restart it, as if he had forgotten to change the previous one, until today. Any vestige of my arrival should now be being recorded over.

Next the jumble, as Stuart had called it. Just before my disappearance I'd happened to mention there had been some sort of infestation and rot in my apartment block. Although my rooms were not affected, I was warned there would be a lot of dust as they removed most of the plastered surfaces to get at old timbers and there would fumigation fumes rising from below. They advised me to cover everything I could, so I was thinking of finding one of those lock-up placed to store my good clothes. The kind man offered to keep them in one of his spare rooms for a week or so and I took them over. Now I am arranging them in the wardrobe of the master bedroom – well, shall we say in my half. And I've added a few of my toiletries to the en suite bathroom, plus one or two nick-nacks downstairs. Looks like I've moved in, now.

Final touches, drop my security tag into the wall safe, check on Stuart who is well out of it and breathing a little raggedly, (but he should just about survive until I get back). Finally, to make sure nothing incriminating to me is left behind, I clear away all signs of the coffee and biscuits, and Stuart's drink, don my hoodie, walk to the garage and slowly back out my car, my face shielded from the CCTV.

I did find a few things of Patrycja's in the house, which I threw in a black bag, to be dropped in one of the lidded rubbish bins behind the shopping parade I pass on the way home.

'See you later, Stuart. I'm coming back to save your life.'

Except, something hasn't gone quite to plan. I've arrived back in a taxi to find the flashing blue lights of police cars. Or perhaps it has. I see Patrycja's car there, too.

Four Years Later

●●●

I'm soaking up the sun on a patch of golden sand, a gentle breeze cooling me in the hot summer sun, aqua-blue waves rolling gently ashore, the susurration of pebbles on the main beach bringing a calmness to my thoughts. Just me and my daughter, two years old, now. I watch her building a sandcastle, running back and forth with a blue bucket to fetch sea water for the moat, which immediately drains away. And she giggles every time. She looks up, smiles. 'Love you Mummy.'

We live down here now. It's a perfect place to bring up a child, with the love and attention I never had. The two of us in nature's harmony. John? That was sad. He never aspired to the higher ranks, happy to plod on chasing petty criminals, always at the beck and call of others. Not really what I hoped for. Then he had the accident. Fatal. Our ride-on mower stalling on the grassy bank behind our old house. Stopping so suddenly it tipped over and rolled on top him. I didn't hear his cries in time. There was nothing the paramedics could do; he'd severed an artery. A surprisingly clean cut, actually, from a dirty old mower.

It was his life assurance that bought my beautiful bungalow by the sea.

●●●

Printed in Great Britain
by Amazon